The Halt during the Chase

Also by Rosemary Tonks

NOVELS

Opium Fogs
Emir
The Bloater
Businessmen as Lovers
The Way Out of Berkeley Square

POETRY

Notes on Cafés and Bedrooms
Iliad of Broken Sentences
Bedouin of the London Evening: Collected Poems

CHILDREN'S BOOKS

On Wooden Wings: The Adventures of Webster
Wild Sea Goose

Rosemary Tonks

THE HALT DURING THE CHASE

A NEW DIRECTIONS PAPERBOOK

Manufactured in the United States of America
First published as a New Directions Paperbook (NDP1576) in 2023
Design by Erik Rieselbach

Library of Congress Cataloging-in-Publication Data
Names: Tonks, Rosemary, author.
Title: The halt during the chase / Rosemary Tonks.
Description: First New Directions edition. |
New York : New Directions Books, 2023.
Identifiers: LCCN 2023016473 | ISBN 9780811237451 (paperback) |
ISBN 9780811237468 (ebook)
Subjects: LCGFT: Novels.
Classification: LCC PR6070.05 H35 2023 |
DDC 823/.914—dc23/eng/20230407
LC record available at https://lccn.loc.gov/2023016473

2 4 6 8 9 7 5 3 1

New Directions Books are published for James Laughlin
by New Directions Publishing Corporation
80 Eighth Avenue, New York 10011

The Halt during the Chase

I

I was that little girl we had been talking about. And the details of her life meant everything to me.

"Yes, there *were* enough of those yellow-cream blouses. But there was never, never, enough underwear."

My mother always clashed the iron when she disagreed with me.

"So hardly done by. I'm surprised you survived it." (Clash) "Those printed boarding-school inventories were for very rich little girls, and you weren't a rich little girl. Two shoe-bags indeed. One regulation blue beach-gown . . ."

Oh that regulation blue beach-gown! I'd nearly forgotten all about it. What a joy to recover it. And no wonder my mother remembered so well. She took it over for herself and used to change inside it on Bournemouth beach.

"That's right. You took it away from your daughter, you greedy mother. But you were paid back by the portholes."

"Armholes."

"*Portholes*, darling. You used to button yourself from the neck down to the ground, and stand there, smiling mysteriously, under the impression that nothing could be seen below decks—sorry, below stairs."

With her head on one side, my mother looked at herself in the past.

"Could you see anything?"

"Oh everything, everything! Much more than there was

really. Because you did things so slowly inside, and when you bent over to take off your wet bathing costume, that changed the angle of the viewing slits, and there wasn't a single bit of you that hadn't appeared twice over by the time you'd finished."

"Mmmm." She seemed pleased. I began to get angry with her, just as I used to down there on the sands.

"I do believe you knew it all the time!"

"Don't be silly."

"Then why were you always laughing when you had it on? People used to come up from all over the beach to find out what was going on 'under the blue robe' with the smiling and laughing-out-loud face above it."

"It was just that—"

"They thought you were one of the 'turns,' you know. Like Houdini getting out of a strait-jacket. If you knew how I suffered! I had to stand in front of first one porthole and then the other, out-staring the crowd, while you showed off your top."

"And sometimes I fell over," said my mother, egging me on in case I forgot something.

"You fell over and lay on the ground, laughing weakly. And we children had to get you up on your feet again, and cover up bits of you with our own towels. You were the most naked covered-up woman I've ever seen."

My mother ironed on serenely, hoping I wouldn't stop. I promptly stopped and hit on a real grudge of my own.

"You remember that term you sent me back with those lengthened vests?"

"No." She was still years back, lying in a weakened condition on Bournemouth beach.

"You hid them in my trunk underneath one ordinary aertex one. You'd crocheted on the tops in *pink* thread and in a feminine design, all holes, really revolting. Well, I found them just before inspection, thank God, and it was 'Death to the Vests' in my soul. They gave me goose-flesh all over just to look at. After that I spent the whole term in that one aertex vest. I used to wash it at night in cold water, hang it under the bed on a piece of string during the night, and put it on wet in the morning."

"You naughty child! You could have got pneumonia."

"Pneumonia any day, rather than wear grafted-on pink opera-tops. You know, darling, I couldn't tell you then but I can tell you now, I knew exactly which day of the term I would begin to be late down to breakfast because of vest-drying, and trying to find a pair of stockings with only one or two holes in them."

"Absolute rubbish! You had dozens of pairs of stockings. I remember darning them."

"That was the trouble. I'd put them on and suddenly—plunk! A toe would go through. And then I'd have to get it back. I'd stand absolutely still and concentrate inside my shoe, and I'd retract it slowly, like a limb from the stocks. And the very moment I'd got it back with the rest of the foot, all warm in the bosom of the family, and was trying to walk very carefully ... like some poor crippled child ... then—plunk! Out it went through another hole I didn't even know existed!"

She wouldn't be won over by the joking way it was told, on account of the slight on her darning. In fact she'd been enjoying the story of the vests because it contained her crochetwork, but there were too many stinging nettles in my reminiscences and I could see she was getting ready to retaliate. It was all pointed against *her*. The ironing board became a barricade.

"Any more complaints?" she asked.

The trouble was I was really enjoying myself, and I knew that she was too. If I didn't go too far it would be all right. All I had to do was to listen to the noise of the iron and to keep my nostrils alert for the slightest smell of singeing. The iron was seething as she went over the damped-down patches of a blouse, and when she got to the seams around the armpits it hissed again softly as it always did when it found water.

"I'm not complaining. I'm just telling you what it was like, now that we're both grown-up and it doesn't matter."

We both knew we weren't grown-up and it *did* matter, and since we were quite wise enough to know this, my remark was a conspiracy between us. This time my mother took the joke and relented.

"Well, I'm very interested to hear all about it." That meant "go on" and pax.

"You know the most important garments at school, darling? The regulation dark blue knickers. And they were knickers too!"

"You had them."

"I know I had them. And I needed them. You see, there was a gym full of torture gear. It had white ropes hanging down, all varnished so you couldn't grip them, parallel bars, a horse with a stuffed leather top, and some great big jute doormats. When we took our tunics off for the gym lesson, you could see exactly what everyone else had on. Girls used to go into corners and pull their tunics up over their heads as though their last hour had come. If you had large bloomers with weak elastic around the legs and waist, you looked like an Elizabethan wearing those loaded bags they wore, and you were forever tucking them in. And if you had small tight bloomers, they might tear, and you dare not do somersaults in them."

"Why didn't you get yourself excused gym?"

"You couldn't. It was compulsory. At boarding-school everything was compulsory or forbidden. But the worst thing of the lot was to have bloomers which were *the wrong shade of blue*. That was a nightmare, because straight away one started looking at such girls, and they always seemed to have oddly shaped legs—funny knees with oyster pieces in the middle of them that wobbled ..."

My mother, who had placed herself at the centre of my story, quickly bent down and lifting her skirt had a good hard look at her knees.

"Oh, yours are all right, darling." The iron went on with its interested seething. "But even worse than the worst thing of the lot," my voice went down, and I found I was almost whispering, "was to go back with *green* bloomers. That was death, suicide, the end *amen*. You might just as well go out and hang yourself with your lacrosse boot-laces from the walnut tree."

"You impossible children!" said my mother. But she was impressed.

"When we saw a girl had green bloomers we knew she was soft in the head." I was surprised to hear myself dropping back into the old schoolgirl jargon. "From then on she was nicknamed 'Batty.' You'd say: 'I say, Batty, catch this,' then you threw her nothing and she tried to catch it, and so on. Which proved conclusively that she was batty, and getting battier every minute."

"Poor child."

"Even when she put her tunic on again, and tried to walk about like a normal human being, it was no good. The fatal colour underneath seemed to go on shining through—idiot green, the colour of brussel sprouts and other groceries. No one but a slave wore it, an outsider of doubtful stock, the sort of person who would tell excruciating jokes—or say: 'Bees in a beehive must be-hive'—or even try to kiss you! It gives me a cold sweat to think of it even now."

"Well, you can thank your mother, whom you don't appreciate, that you weren't tortured like that."

"I know ... but I almost feel as though I *had* been. It was only by the skin of my teeth that you got me the regulation ones. You know, sometimes I'd think: 'Are they blue—or—green?' I was afraid I was colour-blind. I'd rush into the bedroom and root about in the chest of drawers, and stare at them hopelessly. I was so surprised to find that they were blue, they might just as well have been green! Isn't it awful!"

"Hypersensitive little blossom."

"Don't be sarcastic when I'm telling you the truth. That's not fair. I shan't tell you about my blazer now."

"Your blazer? You had a perfectly good blazer." The iron was moving faster and faster up and down the ironing board. If I didn't praise my blazer something would be burnt; we'd have that well-known brown footprint, the dead weight of the iron landing on a blouse or an afternoon teacloth, to show that the abominable snowman had walked that way.

"*I know* I had a good blazer. Next to those damn dark blue knickers, it was the most important single piece of clothing. I loved that breast pocket with the shiny badge on it saying '*Vive Ut Postea Vivas*' or 'Drinks at 6 every evening.' And then those deep pockets in which you carried around your iron rations for dealing with school life: penknives, fivestones, rubber bands, notes in screws of paper, and match-boxes with families of china dogs in them ... Once you had it on, it was like armour plating, it changed your character. You could use bad language, you were brave enough to stand up in a school debate and say 'Friends, Romans, countrymen,' and you could have repartee with *dangerous* girls, years older, in the 6th form."

"Silly little thing!" (So we were safe again!)

"But *without* a blazer you were just a knock-kneed ninny, a milksop weakling in a soft blouse and tunic. Any fool could come along and shove a cold hand down the back of your neck and call out: 'Hullo, Hurst!' and then give one of those screaming laughs, like a doorbell ringing."

"I remember that dreadful noise. Scream! It was like an ambulance ringing the doorbell."

"Exactly. So you see how important a blazer was, darling. And then, in prep, I'd hunch up inside it and colour in some phoney drawing of rock strata with those greasy crayons that found all the lumps in the paper and left white peninsulas ... and the funny thing was, I used to catch sight of one side of my nose, like a great white chalk cliff or a marshmallow, and I couldn't get rid of it. I kept seeing it. God, it was awful!"

My mother shone at me over the ironing board; something boastful had got into her expression. She had a chiselled little nose, much admired for its neat finish above her lips and the fine grain of the skin on it. Other noses turned into doughnuts when she put her chiselled nose down near them. My own nose being much younger, I hoped it was still "developing," that is, shrinking into itself and getting ready to show the chisel, like hers—but she wouldn't have it so. She especially liked to take her nose out in rough winds at the seaside, and when everyone else was tinted up or hung with ice and mosses, her nose remained porcelain hard and tidy, just as it had been when she first set out.

She looked out of the window now, so that I could see it sideways, and pretended to be struck by some marvel of nature—falling leaves or a tabby cat, anything would do. Really! The vanity of it.

It reminded me at once of—yes, the famous pyjamas. There was just time, before I ran to catch the shops, to remind her that chiselled noses do not make good dressmakers. Thus proving that other kinds of noses—well,

"Darling …"

"Yes." She wanted me to go on about noses.

"You made some of my school clothes yourself." This sounded like a compliment and the iron continued its thumping English trochee: *buff; click* (returning to its metal resting place). "I'll never forget the red, white and blue pyjamas. Do you remember? You bought the flannel down at Gaze's from a great big bale that was being sold off cheaply (and I know why!). And you stayed up late at night and mastered the art of pyjama-making all alone with love in your heart and your foot pressed on the pedal of the sewing machine, going along like a provincial train, te-tum te-tum te-tum."

"So I did!"

"And then I caught you trying to smuggle them into my trunk, those Union Jacks."

"I never *smuggled* anything into your trunk."

"Yes, you did. You smuggled in the British flag cut into three impossible pairs of pyjamas."

"Oh!"

"My heart sank like a stone. I couldn't believe it. I nearly cried out: 'You can't do this to me!'"

"Do *what* to you?"

"The way the collars fitted into the neck—you'd sort of wheedled the material around corners against its will. And the lapels turned back in a peculiar way, boy, those lapels! They had a dreadful kind of flair about them; honestly,

Chanel would have started a whole new fashion from the point you turned the lapels back."

"I don't know what—"

"It was daring, daring, daring. Even the button-holing stitch done in red silk, with the stitches so thickly set together that you could hardly get the button through the slit—unless you pushed hard—I saw a term's battiness staring me in the face! I remember I came and *looked* at you, to try to melt you. First I looked at you with a raging stare, then I turned it down to a beseeching supplication."

"What I had to go through with such a child!"

I was looking up at her now, just as I had done all those years ago, and trying to melt down the profile in front of me. And the difficulties had not changed—for here was a face so exactly like my own (and I understood it *better* than my own) that there was no impersonal point—on the brow say, or the chin, or side of the cheek, where I could stick my petition.

My mother was as naughty as I had been, and I couldn't rely on her to play fair. She might start off with some wise grown-up sentencework, but this would quickly become mumbled over by certain other animal noises, sobs or even hiccoughs, brought in to get her out of her difficulties and responsibilities.

Suppose, in those days, I had put *the* question, the one about the *facts of life*? That would have brought about a cataclysm, gastro-enteritis and two days in bed, sipping hot milk. She would probably have ended up by asking *me* about them ... as soon as she felt better and was taking an interest in such things again.

I said:

"You know you were absolutely staggered to think that you'd been able to make the pyjamas at all! I could see it on your face. You kept saying: 'They're almost professional.'

And you turned them over with the greatest possible satisfaction, just like me with my highly-coloured drawing of rock strata!"

My mother drew in a breath fiercely, and wondered which way to take the words. She let it out, and asked with ingenuousness and with defiance:

"What was wrong with them then?"

At that split second she caught my eye over the ironing board and under the clothes hanging down from the drier, and the answer in both our faces was: "Everything."

We immediately started to laugh so infectiously we couldn't stop. My mother held on to the board and went scarlet—and the silliness of the sounds we were making, the nanny-goat bleat or bray, set us off again every time we stopped. I stifled my horrible moans for an instant and nearly ruptured myself because the laughter then started up silently in my stomach and battered its way uphill past obstacles like a great vibrating wave that had to get out or explode and blast off the top of my head.

When it had blown itself out, my mother was left clinging to her ironing board plank, weak, done for, as if shipwrecked, crying in spasms:

"Stop! Stop! Oh my stomach muscles."

We quietened down, switched off the iron, and lifted the fragrant pile of pressed clothes to a safe place, where they wouldn't be laughed over. Then we made a cup of tea, since we were in pieces, and drank it in silence to heal our aching muscles after the severe pounding they'd had. My mother said we'd had our money's worth out of the pyjamas, but even as she said it, she looked at me flirtatiously, still hoping for a compliment for them, after all these years. I knew that this was how she got herself loved (certainly by me), by bamboozling whoever it was, and not giving up.

Yes, she flirted with me, and when I was a child she dressed to please me. The trouble was that I used to respond by adoring her; by kissing her brow, her hands, her neck, by leaving notes sealed with plasticine seals on her pillow at night, telling her that I loved her, so that she could get through the hours of darkness without me. And even by taking care to simulate awkward boyish movements when I dressed myself, sticking out my elbows in sharp angles, so that she could say in one of those "asides" playwriters used to indicate in stage directions: "You should have been a boy, my dear child." And make a gratified chuckle, an interior music that she needed for her happiness. Oh I knew my duties. I mended objects in the house, saucepan lids, broom handles that fell out of their rightful sockets, and broken tea-pot lids that had to be propped together while a brown bubble of glue was sliced off the cut. I did this because I had been told that my father (who was dead) "could do anything with his hands." This phrase, which time has put in perspective (and much too well) and which now irritates me, was of the first importance to my mother. And it was then my duty to give up my whole life to pleasing her. If I was my father's boyish daughter, then I was practically my father, and this fitted us together as a better pair. It apportioned to me the role of basket-carrying husband, moral leader and decision-taker.

When I took up the complementary role with such simplicity, it never occurred to me that such play-acting could harm me in any way, or harm my mother. If only someone had warned us! Sometimes I had a whiff of the chloroform bandages that kept me in the drugged sleep of childhood, bound hand and foot, stupid, loving, dull, and I'd wake up for a minute with the feeling that I was suffocating. When this claustrophobic fit was on me, I'd run to the front door, fling it open and gasp for air. Those are the moments when a voice reaches your ears from deep inside the house: "For heaven's sake close the door, you're letting all the cold air in."

Innocent play-acting is the most dangerous kind, because it's so thorough, and has a clear conscience. Warnings would have been useless on account of our innocence—they would have been dissolved in a solution of Union Jack pyjama laughter. Anything awkward was ridiculed out of existence, and lost its cutting edge.

Deep down at the centre of all this activity, we knew that the one thing we must never put into words—we who were so articulate—was the pact between us to conceal, each one, the childhood of the other. It ran deeper than the useful concealment of my sex, now and again, for the sake of the play. So it was never said that it was my mother who was the child, and myself who was the mother. Most of the time she was a wholly unreliable schoolgirl accomplice of my own age, because, although she was part of me, on account of the blood tie, she was in violent competition with me. And if she should happen to lose over some minor wrangle, a word game or a general knowledge question, I would suddenly find that I had turned into a husband in the middle, married to her, and having to dry her tears on my unspeakable Vb handkerchiefs.

My mother could only be herself so fully in this way when she was in my presence, because I provided her with all the necessary backgrounds: child, mother, and husband. Unfortunately it prevented me from being myself, for in order that she could be "on stage" in my life I must first be "off stage" in that life.

There was a third catch to these manoeuvres, and that was that occasionally my mother played at being my mother. This took us both so completely unawares that I would stand gazing at her, turned to granite. I remember these moments as desperate, connected with injustices so gigantic I nearly fell to the ground under the mental disorganisation as I tried to assimilate them into my moral brain. Out of our depth, we floundered, not knowing any of the usages of this *real* situation. And we simply had to wait until the mood passed and we could "be ourselves" again.

She was putting on her hat.

"Quickly. The shops."

My God, yes. The shops and my mother's hats went together. She was doing what she had done for the last thirty years, pulling out certain pieces of hair and pushing in certain other pieces, as though getting ready for Botticelli. Nothing makes a woman angrier or more grown-up. My mother's voice produced a mezzo-soprano tone, as though she suddenly had a layer of bark on her voice-box. At the same time she gave herself really nasty looks in the spotted hall mirror. When she was ready I would have to come in with noises of appreciation like a 'cello giving loyal groans. *Those* were the moments of injustice, of assumed motherhood, when the words went on running out of her mouth. My mother always made a terrific noise in front of a mirror; if she had nothing to say, she would huff and puff as she fought with her image.

"You should have been grateful that you had a mother to do all those things for you. Instead of finding fault."

"Oh I was."

"It doesn't sound like it." She looked more kindly at the mirror and her voice lost that "on and on" sound. "There!" She made a absolutely appalling face into the mirror, and turned around to me, smiling and pretty in a brown feathered bird-hat that made her look sweet enough to eat. "Like it?"

"Love it. You look like Rudi's thrush."

"Don't mention that man to me!"

"Oh piffle, you adore him."

"Not content with stealing all my birds for his bird table by putting out Dundee cake, he's writing me horrible letters."

"That sounds like love—that fiery tone you're using."

"He's either persecuting women or flirting with them. There's nothing in between. Very unbalanced. No wonder he can't keep a marriage going. Read that letter on the hall table."

It was jammed back into its envelope, and the envelope was an expensive affair lined with red tissue. I took it out and read: "*Angela, my darling …*"

"He sounds friendly enough—"

"Read on. It's so incongruous. First the 'darling' then the complaints."

I read aloud:

"Could you possibly do something about your central heating fumes? It's like living next door to an oil refinery. I can't face breakfast on my balcony any more and I am afraid that I shall lose Mrs Wynne. You know she always leaves her grandchild outside in the pram? She says the fumes are so bad that she is afraid they may affect him, and prevent him developing properly. Just come over and smell them for yourself. I assure you that when the wind's blowing in this direction …"

"Stunting Mrs Wynne's grandchild!"

"I know!" My mother's eyes, normally dark brown, were absolutely black with pleasure.

Rudi was Rudolf Horner, and he had the enormous house and garden next door to my mother's cottage in Hampstead. He ran a firm of antique dealers, auctioneers and furniture removers, and was wealthy enough to do exactly what he wanted, which included divorcing two wives; each of them had a son by him. Now that his first wife was dead, his second lived only two streets away with her child, Guy, whom I knew so well. Guy was only twenty-two and I, at thirty-one, knew him as personally as I knew my mother and was as casual with him as if he was myself. The reason was simple: I was in love with Philip—half-brother to Guy and the child of the first marriage. Hampstead families are very close, and if they don't actually intermarry, someone in one family is in love with someone in another all their lives. It was difficult to get on with the next stage of this love-affair of mine, because we all knew each other so well and it seemed to take the urgency out of it. And then, in spite of being a quiet man, a thinker, he was the son of Rudolf Horner, who was, after all, well ... Look at this letter. It was almost as funny as my mother's Union Jacks. And if I looked doubtfully at Philip's father, wasn't he doing the same to my mother? And yet his father was *my type*, and I got on perfectly with him.

I had the impression that Philip was "thinking me over" at the moment, and although this incited me to prodigious actions—it turned me into a beauty with long fair hair, because I *had* to be one—pieces of grit were finding their way into my pride. I loved desperately, but my mind grew saner every day. Unbelievably, I could even begin to see ahead of me a point which I might pass, imperceptibly, and beyond which I would not want to live with him, although I could not necessarily stop myself loving him. But the sun was still rising between us; if he allowed me to get to that point, and to go past it, then he wanted it. Philip *knew* me. We had passed that stage when all hearts are opened and all secrets known; he knew my timing, my morality, my values, my income, my family background, my age, my body. And while we met, and met again, and again, we were entirely happy as the barometer rose steadily ... but nothing was said.

This made me uneasy. I, myself, was in no hurry. And this was because I had a feeling that if we married, I would be perpetually anxious, not because he would be unfaithful, but because I would always be too much in love. I certainly didn't want to run ahead into that state. So I waited for him to speak ... in the exact bureaucratic terminology of marriage ... meanwhile getting torn while I resisted the magnet between us and getting blinded by the great spectacles which day—and night—dreaming lit up on the screen inside my head.

My mother, who was on her own side in this matter, used to prick me with: "How's it going?" So childish, so shrewish, that I had to answer on the same level: "How's what going?" She would then draw her face into an expression of nauseating complicity, just like a mime who only has one second to portray some human failing and so has to do it with decisive vulgarity. Heaven knows what underworld theatre she got the expression from, but it was invaluable. It so put me off my great love that I could push him aside for up to an hour, two hours, just as I had during the conversation about my old school clothes. And with any luck I could add a third hour of free mental time for myself, by reminding myself that he was the son of Rudolf Horner, who was ... one of our oldest, most amusing friends.

2

That crumpling-clinking noise was the sound the old front door made as it shut behind us on two locks and rang the bit of chain which is provided for linking the door to the frame when you hold it just open to talk to burglars.

We were still in a good humour, enjoying the winter day. I stood by Mother while she sniffed the air outside her cottage. She said anxiously:

"I can't smell anything. Can you?"

"Central heating fumes."

She looked at me with completely round eyes and brows lifted roundly above them; I'd never seen such a bird-hatted circle of a face.

"No, of course not! Your little cottage couldn't make enough fumes to go as far as Rudi's. It's probably the church."

"I'll switch it off tonight, and I'll write him a note: *You're letting an old woman freeze to death ...*"

"No, darling, you mustn't go down to his level. Or before you know it you'll find yourself married to him."

"That'll be the day!" my mother said boldly, looking up and down the street in case someone came out and tried to marry her. "Huh."

"I don't see why you shouldn't marry him. He's got nice skin."

"You must be joking." She was very nearly sharp, and I wondered why.

"I don't see anything wrong with him," I said, without thinking. "What's wrong with him?"

It was my turn to catch her eye, as it had been her turn over the ironing board. And the answer I got was the same one: *Everything!*

We were able to keep up our musical comedy turns along a rather boring piece of road. And we were entering an infinitely more exciting stretch, almost dangerously pickled with past events, when I saw Guy, back from Paris, talking to Mr Ruback in the distance.

"Uhuh. There's Guy with his Sufi teacher."

My mother stopped telling me about the way she had "bagged" my father in marriage with no real powder on her face, only prepared chalk, and looked over the two figures comprehensively.

"Not at all like a Jehovah's Witness."

"Not in the least."

"But he has got light eyes."

"Lovely. Like martini poured in."

"His chin juts out a bit."

"It does."

"That shows intolerance in a man. He's probably difficult."

"Almost certainly. He's changed Guy's whole life." I hesitated. And then pretending to myself that there was no chasm ahead of me, I said in the briefest way I could: "And he's beginning to change mine."

"*Yours?*"

Oh you idiot! Why on earth do you have to say such things to your mother? A word once let out of the cage, says Horace, cannot be whistled back again. Now for it.

"Yes. Mine." Looking away.

"What does that mean?"

I was just sighing deeply when, with the intensest relief, I suddenly remembered that I was thirty-one and entitled to my own life. All I had to do was to take it. What do you owe your mother? Mumbled words or a full, rational explanation? I gave her a crumbling mouthful of this and that:

"Everything he says seems true. He teaches you ... how to live. Answers big questions."

"What sort of questions?" She was very curious and pretending to be naïve so that she could get her fingers on more "facts of life."

I didn't reply at once—and all the time we were getting closer—because she'd irritated me by bringing my huge, vague, clean answer down to some pettifogging level, some sexual level as humdrum as a dishcloth. There were times when she played the bourgeois like this, by being a little too avid for a certain kind of information, and I would shut up house like a clam. She had a quick look into my face, and noting her mistake, she rapidly made it up:

"I see. The eternal questions, time, space, matter, and so forth."

She hadn't dropped her voice, but had arranged it perfectly, because we were abreast of them. Guy was smiling slightly at both myself and Mr Ruback, who was in a courteous shape giving the whole of his attention to the boy in front of him, as freshly as though they were meeting for the very first time. I knew that he had heard the words, and would nod to us, and that there would not even be a hint over the whole of his person that he had heard *those* words in *that* tone of voice from a similar source a hundred times before. There would not even be a distilled, animal weariness in the turning of his head. I wanted Mr Ruback to be perfect; but I had raised my standards so inexorably for him that he was bound to be found out, to be human and to fail and irritate me sooner or later. And that would allow me to escape from his teaching, if I found subsequently that it was inconvenient, or if I became lazy. So I raised him higher every minute, and was doing it right then.

I noticed he was dressed as usual in formal, dark consulting-room clothes. But the good quality of his attire was directly related to his controlled manner. I remember one night he did an extremely funny imitation of an accident-prone man-letting his arms fly out from their sockets, his head wag off dottily to one side, and loosening the muscles of his lower lip so that it poked out as if it was part of a milk jug. It was so convincing that you would have said he had changed into an old creased suit for the act, put on a dirty shirt, and certainly needed his hair to be cut straight away. (It was thick grey hair, expensively chopped in decent manly clumps like a privet hedge.) Inside *this* Harley Street specialist there was a court jester.

Walking past the two of them normally, took us all our strength. I saw everything in such vivid colours, my chest was blocked up with unexploded air—I suppose I was holding my breath, in case something went wrong. I could even hear my own ears ringing, as we got by without a scratch as though by-passing a spiritual ambush.

My mother seemed exhausted by it too. She straightened her hat as people straighten pictures on a wall after an earthquake. I knew that when she attended to her hat something important had happened. It occurred to me that she found Mr Ruback attractive and might even be considering "bagging" him in marriage. To my surprise she turned to me and hissed decisively:

"You're right! He *is* psychic."

She was flustered. And to calm herself she opened her bag and took from a box a scented pellet of sugar. On the box it said: "Flower-scented cachous prepared from the choicest ottos." She ate the cachou (which smelt like bath salts) and was at once better. In no time her own psyche—which had had to take second place to Mr Ruback's on the pavement—rose up and began to twitter; but sweetly and harmlessly.

"In some ways he reminds me of your father—the nice clean neck, I suppose. And there's a look of Michael Morgan," naming a Harley Street doctor who was in favour at the moment.

At once I saw what she was up to. He frightened her. She wanted to relate him to other men of a similar age whom she knew, in order to feel more at home with him. As soon as she had fitted him into her Rogues' Gallery, and if possible had some repartee with him, she would be able to relax.

While she turned him over in her mind and bevelled off the awkward bits which stuck out and were incomprehensible to her, she went over her last "interview" with Michael Morgan in her search for similarities. She had summed Morgan up from the opposite side of his desk, put her own philosophy of life, tried to winkle out his, and then had thrown some red herrings across the trail of her symptoms to test the diagnosis. He was:

"... a perfect pet. How different from that dreadful creature who held up his hand and said 'Stop!' when I tried to describe my habits."

Morgan had not made the mistake of thinking that my mother was being trivial when she said, for example, that she had stopped eating Oat-Crunchies because she was sure they gave her wind. He had the wit to see that she knew how to make her life interesting, and was prepared to do the same for other lives; Mr Ruback also looked the sort of person who would listen to my mother's ideas on Oat-Crunchies, and would realise that this was the unique way she put over the message of her doubts and anxieties about my future and her own.

At the end of the road I turned for a last look back. They were in exactly the same attitude, like two waxworks from Madame Tussaud's, a man and a boy eternally discussing the secret of life. As it happened, I was to hear later from Guy that he was describing to Mr Ruback his encounter with the ghost of Baudelaire who had passed him as he crossed one of the bridges of the Île St Louis at eleven twenty-five one night last summer. This extraordinary story, which can be told in broad daylight and still make you shiver, was rooting them to the paving stones. And Guy told me that he kept repeating to Mr Ruback: "I didn't know he wasn't alive. *How can you tell when it is a ghost?*"

I bought myself a rump steak at the butcher's, and then left my mother to go back to my own flat. We did not live together; we were far too similar. Besides, I was afraid of the dependent relationship re-forming. Every now and again when this old fear got hold of me, I could be boorish. I, who loved her company, could turn on her and say pointedly: "Don't fascinate *me*. I'm not your husband, you know." "Same old Sophie!" was the fierce reply.

I left her with the briefest kiss, almost in the middle of a sentence, like a boy without manners. I was afraid of being held, even for a second, in a pair of arms which had complete power over me. Then I suddenly decided that I needed more air to get rid of the emotion I felt for her, which ran over my whole body.

I went to the edge of Hampstead Heath and started off towards the Vale of Health. As soon as the wind touched my face I was invigorated, and found myself humming. The Heath was like a great bag of water underfoot on either side of the gravel walks. With the first frosts, the water turned to cast iron. The Heath's great beauty lay in smoothly rounded hills and hillocks with groups of trees on top of them. When the mower circled these in summer and left the shiny wild grass lying on its side, children and dogs ran to bathe in it and for some reason it made them shout and laugh. I would remember my old country skills at such times, the ability to *vanish* by controlling your chemistry and making it receptive so that you could enter the natural world on its own terms, the ability to climb any tree instantaneously, the necessity to wear light foot-gear ...

Today everything was tea-brown. People were taking their dogs home. You could hear boots squelching. There was a soggy bank of ruts turned blue by the sky. Oh, I knew now why I had been talking about my schooldays with my mother. I had gone into the past to avoid the present. Philip was the present.

I now saw that the reason I'd left my administration job at the Languages School in Knightsbridge was because I wanted to be available to see him during the day, and to get my flat done up, so as to make it more attractive to him, and to have time to improve my own appearance. I knew I had to keep up a certain style in order to attract Philip. He hated anything that wasn't quite right. But then, nothing ever is. Anyway, I'd decided to live on my savings for a few months. All this was revealed to me as I went around a big mud puddle on three or four tufts of grass. Why did I pretend to myself I was in no hurry? Everything was right; we met physically and mentally as equals ... but what was that stone-cold pool of thought that suddenly collected inside the living red-blooded heat of my head when certain remarks of his dropped into my mind without warning? Remarks like: "I need a rich wife." And the remark he made on entering my large, rather beautiful flat for the first time: "Oh. I hoped it would be the perfect flat." He was an emotional and impulsive man, in spite of the quiet, steady habits; he would take up with new political causes and worship at new shrines so long as they were at the current centre of world thought and action. If he was sometimes too up-to-date I had no right to be disturbed by this when he was so loyal to me. We were completely faithful to one another, and I discussed everything with him. He made time to listen to me, took pleasure in it, and gave sound advice. He was my best friend, and my perfect lover. Those cold thoughts were the result of looking for trouble.

Quickly. More air! I couldn't get enough of it—I wanted a cold, flowing river of it past my cheeks. Drink it down, white stuff, and get rid of all the vinegar inside you that makes you trembling and irresolute, afraid that you're not rich enough for your lover, whom you love too much on one level and doubt on another.

⋆ ⋆ ⋆

"Pussy! Pussy! You look fantastic."

A growl from the sofa.

"It's the brooch with the slab of green marble in it."

A tea-cup clattered this time. Really I was raining down compliments on her, but they were all true.

Princess Melika, Guy's godmother, was giving us tea in her flat. My mother sat slightly apart, brooding, because I was giving the Pussy too much admiration. She was better at life than my mother; whereas my mother was an enchantress, Melika was a fascinator. And the two dark queens usually sat on different sofas in the same room. Melika won the battle of the sofas because she couldn't care less, and because she cheated and used dogs and people and plants to help her. And if her audience stopped looking at her she would go on with the show for herself alone. Whereas if people stopped looking at my mother it was a serious matter, and I would have to get up and do something about it. Melika had extricated herself, first from Russia, and then from Paris, and it was during that lifetime's journey that she had learnt to live for herself.

Today she was dug into an enormous yellow velvet chesterfield which was all "body," and which I thought had belonged to my Philip's mother while she was alive. I was once told that it had been left to Rudolf Horner, so what it was doing underneath Melika I didn't know. She kept patting and stroking it, so I guessed it was on loan, and she was making a strong bid to possess it, before Rudi got it away from under her. Her little Yorkshire terrier was snoozing comfortably at the other end, as though lying in yellow sunlight on Hampstead Heath.

My mother mournfully described some of her recent symptoms, which had forced her into the hands of a trichologist.

"I was so overwrought, it affected my hair. Masses fell out. And the first thing he said when he took hold of my head was: 'This is the smallest head I've had through my hands for the last ten years.'"

"The size of the head has nothing to do with it," said Pussy, who had a large head. "You can be intelligent even if your head is the size of a pin."

"I've always known I had a neat, bony little head like a cricket ball," said my mother, keeping on course. "Apparently other people have got great big heads."

"I remember Ziz had quite a small head," said Pussy,

"and you couldn't find anyone more intelligent. He spoke German, French, Spanish, Italian, Russian, Hindi, and heavens knows how many varieties of colloquial Tibetan. Had to! To get out of the sort of scrapes he got into!" She laughed heartily.

"He banged my head about like an old broom," said my mother. "And then he poured on some icy cold stuff and said: 'Does it tingle?'"

"When Ziz was working as a British agent in Turkistan, he had to be ready to change his disguise at a moment's notice. So it wasn't just a matter of languages," said Pussy sternly, "it was concerned with the *whole personality*."

"I said: 'Not a bit, if you want to know the truth!' He didn't like that very much," said my mother, deeply satisfied.

"You know, men of his sort don't have enormous orang-outang skulls ..." Pussy was slowing down as if overcome by the discoveries she was making among her own memories. Without warning she called out gaily: "Look! I'll show you." And she got up and went off to a corner cupboard.

This was definitely unscrupulous, because my mother was left in the middle of a story, with nobody to interrupt her and pretend they were talking on the same subject. And besides we had to wait, because obviously something was going to be shown to us, and we ourselves hadn't brought any exhibits to claim the attention of the court.

Melika came back with a book bound like a heavy photograph album. Inside were pages of hand-made cream paper as thick as the flesh on a human shoulder with the watermark of a vaccination blemish on it. She opened it at the centre and gave us a thrilling look over the top—light green eyes that slid to and fro and must have taken their tint from the waves on some Yalta beach—a little girl as full of mischief as the Black Sea.

"There!"

"Where? ... What is it?"

My mother couldn't find much on the page at all. She was looking for a photograph of Carter, the famous Colonel Carter, C.I.E., preferably with a small bony skull just like her own. Instead of that—nothing ... just a wild flower of some sort which had been pressed between the pages, and which had left a transfer of part of itself on the facing page, a blue wet-mark, a carbon from a petal. Under the shrivelled flower someone had written in Indian ink, with a name-tape pen: *Meconopsis betonicifolia carteri.*

"If that doesn't give you inspiration, nothing will," said Pussy with thunder in her vowels and more sea-tinted lightning in her eyes. "The Blue Poppy of Tibet!"

I felt it was my duty to fall down, slain, on the carpet.

"Is that it?" asked my mother vaguely, as though she had been looking for it, not very hard, in her garden only yesterday.

"It certainly is. He was exploring the mystery of the Tsangpo gorges when he discovered it. He picked it—"

"Oh he shouldn't have done that!" said my mother involuntarily. After all she could never bear to pick her own flowers.

"And brought it to *me*: the famous Tibetan Blue Poppy. And the marvellous thing is that he found it by chance, almost incidentally, while he was risking his life in that terrible, mountainous country. But he had the knowledge to recognise it, of course." Pussy sat down with her album, gloating but reverent. "Do you know what I think?"

"No, Pussy. Do tell us."

"*Nature revealed herself to him,*" said Pussy, so dramatically that I shivered, feeling the wind from those gorges touch the back of my neck. "And that was because his soul was as light as a feather; he had no *baggage*," said Pussy derisively, getting even deeper into the rich yellow back of the sofa. "No worldy goods, no personal ambition, no axes to grind. He travelled light," holding on to the substantial arm of the sofa, "and so he could *see*. He was unified with the natural phenomena around him. He wasn't a stranger in the world as you and I are. If you're that sort of person, you're given things."

"And he was given the blue poppy?"

"Yes, that was his reward. He was the only fully developed human being I have ever met. He was like a god."

"Pussy!"

"Yes, I know what I'm saying ... they named the poppy after him, and he was given the Royal Geographical Society's Gold Medal. Not that that meant anything to him!" Pussy gave one of her Blüthner growls and the light in her eyes changed once more; it was like a torch left on underwater now. Growl!

"You don't have to go to Tibet to pick the blue poppy," said my mother firmly, trying to dismiss the excess magic.

"He was *here*," said Pussy, for once making a mistake and picking up the temporal thread.

"Where?" I looked over my shoulder.

"We walked together on Hampstead Heath, down the broadwalk ... in those days it was kept very neatly, just like the Bois de Boulogne."

"What did you talk about?"

"Nothing. We were very peaceful. I remember someone had caught a large pike in one of the ponds—the big one up towards Highgate. I can see it now, in beautiful condition, it really shone with health. It was a yellowish-brown with dark brown Chinese markings."

"The very day that you and he walked out!"

"Things always happened like that with Ziz."

"What did he look like?"

"Well, he had quite a big nose ..."

"Ah, I'm glad to hear that," said my mother, back on her favourite subject. "A woman's nose has to be small and neat. But a man is quite different. If a man hasn't got a good nose, he should sit down and grow himself one, because he's going to need it! I'm glad to hear he had a good old boko on him."

"Well, I wouldn't say that exactly ..." Pussy was uneasy because she knew my mother was out to humanise her god, and might try to make him ridiculous.

"I remember one Jewish family in which the men had little tiny noses. And they had to go out and get themselves wives with great big noses, and breed them in again," said my mother.

Melika gripped her brooch, afraid the conversation was getting away from her and becoming flippant. She thought herself to be Jewish, as much as anyone can ever be said to be Jewish, and being very well-bred, she was afraid that my mother might remember this and be embarrassed. So she quickly changed the conversation, and turning to her asked her whether she had any news of Guy in Paris.

"He's back. We saw him last week," said my mother. "He was looking a bit wild because of his hair on his shoulders, but otherwise quite nice in a sort of long military coat. I don't know what he's doing, living in Paris on his own. Won't give Biddy or any of us his address."

"*I* have his address," said Pussy in full majesty. "I gave him a lot of advice when he was going over to live there, and he writes to me regularly. I said: 'If you're going over to study the French cuisine, avoid the Crillon if you want good cream of asparagus soup, because they always burn it there.'"

She gave us this piece of information as though it was equal in importance to her talk on Colonel Carter, the explorer. She might just as well have said: "If you're going to Tibet, avoid the Tsangpo gorges because the wind is really bitter there." Obviously she didn't see the incongruity either in this, or in giving such a piece of advice to Guy, who was living on a pittance and might be quite glad to have a night's work in the kitchens of the Crillon.

It wasn't that Melika lived richly, it was simply that this was the level on which she did her observing, thinking and commenting. And so convincing, so solidly welded together, was her personality, that good cream of asparagus soup did, for the moment, seem as important to all of us as the quest for the incredible blue poppy.

At that second her old maid, Kate (old Funny-Cuffs), opened the door and in came Guy's mother, Biddy Horner, late and panting.

"Oh I'm so sorry. I'm too late. Everything's gone."

Biddy was a full-blown hurrying little woman with high colouring and bouncing permed fair hair. I'm sure she had caught Rudi with her gushing confident head and driven him away by sitting in a chair and watching him with as much animation as if she was still talking. She made Melika look very foreign and her dark wavy hair which grew in locks, tendrils, and what one can only call "pieces," suddenly went black.

"Biddy," said Pussy. "Where is Guy?"

"He's locked up in his room at home. I can't get him out. He just reads or sleeps. He says he's 'preparing' himself. I'm worried to death about him."

"Aha!" said Pussy, absolutely delighted with him. "Exactly what I did at his age."

Biddy was staggered; it turned out that her son was doing exactly the right thing, and that she, Biddy, wasn't going to get any sympathy. She made another effort to put him in the wrong.

"I tried to get him to come with me, Pussy. I'm terribly sorry ..."

"Completely unimportant," said Pussy, wiping it off the face of the earth with a forthright hand-signal to all of us, rather as if she were trying to park the yellow sofa and wanted plenty of room. "Let Guy be himself. I won't have him bullied."

Kate brought in fresh tea, the Yorkshire terrier woke up, and suddenly there seemed to be crumbs all over the place. It was something to do with the way Biddy panted, because I remembered that when she came to tea with us there seemed to be almost enough cake crumbs left over on the sofa afterwards to make a whole new cake.

Melika wanted me to talk to her, and was already looking at me with her deep look and saying "How's Philip?" But that was the last thing I wanted to do, and I pretended to be involved in my mother's conversation. At least Biddy was getting a good helping of sympathy there: my mother also had a difficult child which wouldn't do exactly what she wanted it to do. Biddy said to her:

"He seems to have a persecution complex. He says he doesn't want to answer the front door because people keep eating him up. And the books he reads! I wanted to *understand* him, so I went to the library and got hold of one of them, *Ulysses* by James Joyce. And I took the trouble to read it through, right down to the glug-glug-glug gog-gog-gog bits."

"I didn't know there were any glug-glug-glug gog-gog-gog bits," my mother said in a puzzled voice.

"There's nothing else," said Biddy, very worried.

"But surely Guy's got his head screwed on the right way?"

"He was perfectly all right before he met this man."

"What man?" asked my mother, who knew perfectly well and was longing to talk about him.

"A Mr Ruback."

"Ah. So he's a wolf in sheep's clothing!"

"... a totally unknown person in our midst. And when I asked where were these so-called lectures, he flatly refused to tell me! I said: 'I have a perfect right to go on my own account. You can't withhold information from me.'"

"But I've seen this man standing in the street, and there's nothing particularly special about him," said my mother, who thought that if you'd seen someone and knew them, you knew everything about them. She had conveniently forgotten her own agitation as she passed him. The point about Mr Ruback was that until you'd heard his teaching, you didn't know him *at all*, any more than you knew a poet until you'd read his work. So that in reality to know such people for a second in the street was, very nearly, not to know them at all.

Suddenly my mother remembered that I, too, had been to these sinister lectures. She said loudly:

"Just a minute. I want to ask Sophie something. Sophie, will you please explain to us how you suddenly became so *convinced* of—whatever it is you're convinced of?"

A trap. A trap. I looked to Melika for help, but she just nodded to me in a friendly way.

"I—didn't have to be convinced."

"Well!" My mother and Biddy looked around to see if there were any more witnesses to my case, which was a hopeless one; it was obvious I believed anything anyone cared to tell me. I went on:

"No! That's the whole point. You don't have to be *con-*

vinced because you recognise straight away that this is the truth."

The two faces were dismayed. Biddy stubbed out a cigarette with lipstick on it, and suddenly turned to my mother. As though at a signal, they rose together and said they must go. I'd never before seen them so unanimous. They trotted out, ensemble, with their hats on, and I guessed they were plotting. Not only had they recognised a danger—an unseen force had come into their midst and got hold of their children—but they were definitely going to do something about it.

3

"Stay on a minute," said Pussy. "Vodka?"

"No-o. Um. Um. Whisky and ice, please."

"Don't get masculine, child!"

"Don't pretend you're old, Puss!"

"Well, I *am* compared with you."

"You are *not* compared with me."

"Did you like my poppy?"

"I loved it. I'm bowled over, you know that. Pussy, do you believe everyone has to have a cause then? Something unattainable which they must yearn after?"

"Something they must and can attain. I hate foggy ideas. I'm practical. But I'll tell you something: do it all in a sophisticated way. Or they'll make fun of you."

"Have I told them too much already?"

"Well ... be careful. Don't forget. They've got nothing else to do."

"Damn."

"And there are two of them now."

"Tell me more about your life, Pussy."

"I can't. There's too much. It's all Russian roulette: sometimes I had to be dead for two, three, years at a time. Has Philip asked you?"

"Oh Pussy!"

"He hasn't! Not at all like his father, who never does anything else. Go away, then. Go to Paris. No; Normandy. I have some friends near Alençon."

"I don't want to force him—"

"Nothing in this world or the next could force Philip."

"You don't like him?"

"Yes—I do. I do very much. If I were your age I would be in love with him."

"You don't think we're right for one another?"

"Yes, yes. But what's holding him back? If you're going to get married, do it straight away. The sooner the better. While you're still prepared—to make sacrifices. Before you—go on to other things, *in your mind*."

"That's what I'm afraid of."

"Then it's all over!"

"Don't say that!"

I felt the tears dripping down beside my nose, hot and soaking wet.

"Please, please, don't say a thing like that. It frightens me so."

"I'm only telling you what you already know."

"But I don't want to hear it! ... in case it's true."

"Listen to me. He's a very nice man, he's handsome and he can afford you. Now. He's yours if you want him."

I went on snuffling, rather resentful and rather grateful. The next minute I was smiling at her, happier because she'd forced her way into my thoughts and cauterized the bleeding.

Kate knocked on the door confidentially, and after a pause Melika called out: "You can come in." As though she knew who was there. And in came Rudolf Horner.

He was not as tall as his sons, but brilliantly alive with handsome tinted flesh and receding curly grey hair. He was nervous, susceptible, mercurial, able to rise and fall to all levels, preferred running to walking, and acted everything out in front of you.

"And who am I surprising this afternoon!" he said, whirling around and taking in the tea and drinks trays.

"No one, you booby! Vodka?"

"No-o. I think a little whisky, just neat if you don't mind. Ah. How is everybody?"

"We were perfectly all right ..." Pussy began warningly.

"Yes, you were perfectly all right, and then I came in and you felt a great deal better. Isn't that it?"

Silence. He began to laugh.

"All right. I give in. I surrender. Just let me sit down beside you." He sat down on the sofa, and leaned ardently towards Melika. "Oh those eyes, those eyes. Why do they look at me like that?"

"They don't," said Pussy.

"Oh but they do. Don't they, Sophie? Pussy's eyes go down to the bottom of your soul and scour it out, like an old saucepan. No more! One glance is enough to last me all night."

He tried to recline, but couldn't get into a comfortable position. Finally he propped his head on Melika's shoulder, and closed his eyes.

"What's this wet stuff?" asked Pussy, touching his coat jacket. "It's absolutely saturated."

"Oh. Ah. My coat. I had to bend down in your garden, as it happened."

"What for?" She was suspicious.

"Well—I—heard some voices. And so naturally I didn't want to have a collision. I thought I'd have a look around the garden."

"You went and crouched down in the front garden because you heard Biddy's voice?"

"I heard her voice rasping on, and another much sweeter voice, like an angel's ..."

"That wasn't what you said in your letter to her," I said.

"What letter? I know of no letters."

"You said her central heating fumes were stunting Mrs Wynne's grandchild." I put it to him forcefully.

"So I did! I'd forgotten all about it."

"You said it was like living next door to an oil refinery."

"So it was!" He laughed with joy. "It *was*, my dear. When the wind was blowing in my direction, I could hardly breathe. It was like the rain of hot ashes on Pompeii. Honestly. It was like Vesuvius and an oil refinery all rolled into one. You don't *know* what it was like."

"And all the time it wasn't her central heating at all. It was the church's."

"All right then. It was the church's. I don't mind which it was. I only wanted to have a little bit of conversation with your mother. Is there anything so wrong in that?"

"And so you wanted to get her over to your house on the pretext of smelling some fumes—which weren't hers?"

"No, I should hope not."

He was in such a ludicrous mood, refused to get off Pussy's shoulder, and was altogether so funny that we all three switched off into a good-humoured silence. His eyes closed again.

Rudi began to stroke the back of the sofa, just as Melika had done. After a moment, he opened his eyes and stared intently at the velvet. Then he sat himself up and after getting off the sofa, stood back from it and frowned slightly. Melika kept absolutely still, like an animal trying to blend in with its surroundings.

"My dear Pussy, isn't this the sofa that poor Muriel left me?"

"Is what? Sorry, I wasn't listening ..."

"This chesterfield. It's the one Muriel left me in her will."

Melika looked at it, surprised, full of pain, and tried to concentrate.

"I really don't know ..."

"Well, I *do* know. It's my chesterfield."

"I don't know *whose* it is. It's been sitting in my north room covered with dust-sheets for the last ten years, and I thought it was high time I took it out and made it earn its keep. Otherwise I should have to charge storage on it!"

"Humph. If it's in your way, I should be only too pleased to remove it for you."

"It's not so much *in the way*—although I must admit it is cumbersome and bulky—as difficult to integrate into a sitting-room due to its absurd colour."

"Pussy darling, I'll take it away from you. I can see that it's a nuisance to you, and as you say, you may have to charge me storage."

"If you insist on taking it, take it. Though I really don't know who it belongs to. All I know is that it was thick with dust and woodworm and heaven knows what, and I rescued it and refurbished it."

Rudi had begun striding to and fro.

"You see, Pussy, how I know *instantly* that this is my sofa, is quite simple—"

"My dear Rudi, why should you have to justify yourself? I know that sometimes I get an idea into my head, and, rightly or wrongly, I hang on to it, convinced that it's the truth."

"No, you see, in my case it's quite simple. I wouldn't even have noticed it if I hadn't lain on it in that particular attitude—it's amazing really—with my head on your shoulder, like a little dog. And then I began to stroke the velvet, just as I used to all those years ago—before Philip was born!"

"The *same* velvet?"

"Perhaps it has been re-covered over the years: who knows? But it's the same colour, the same horrible yellow ... only in those days it used to be a great deal yellower. It really hurt your eyes." He shaded his eyes. "I remember the first time I saw it ..."

"Nobody doubts your word."

"Muriel was living in Montpelier Square at the time. You may not believe it—but I was madly in love with her—"

"Of course we believe it."

"Well, I came in one day and there was this brand-new chesterfield in the middle of the sitting-room. She called it her 'yellow divano.' You couldn't see anything else in the room. No sign of the old sofa. It was like losing an old friend, a comfortable, reliable friend. You could get *in* to the old sofa, it was just like a boat."

"And you'd both go sailing away, you and Muriel!"

Rudi looked wary.

"On the old sofa, yes. But not on this one." He wanted to get it absolutely clear.

"I must say I wouldn't have bought this particular colour myself ..."

Melika had stepped straight into the trap. Rudi was so pleased, he talked faster than ever.

"Muriel had it covered with this velvet which made a mark if you sat on it. And you had to sit bolt upright, as if you were going to play the piano. And there was *no room*."

"You were frightened of it," said Pussy, settling down inside the trap to make the best of things.

"Yes, I was." I'd never seen Rudi so serious.

By that time there was no doubt in anyone's mind that Rudi had established ownership with an emotional, well-told, and very convenient set of memories. It was right that a man with so many sofas, armchairs, occasional tables, tallboys, chiffoniers, cupboards and desks, should have one more. And this was, after all, Melika's opportunity to get rid of some of her "baggage" and travel light.

Since they had taken up with an old story from the past, I was restless, wanted modern life, and left them. I plunged into the winter night which had come up to the doorstep, vast, dry and very dark, and ran to make my own life.

* * *

I was to have dinner with Philip at his club. Then the plan was that we should drive out of London and put up at a country hotel for the night, get up reasonably early the following morning (Philip was very good at this) and arrive in Northampton about midday. Philip was to give a talk at a public school nearby on "Social Security's New Look." We were then to visit friends of his who farmed, inspect cattle and methods, and drive back slowly talking it all over. This itinerary, as sensible and dull as a pair of galoshes, was relaxed by comparison with many of Philip's organised weekends. The dullness was curious, because Philip seemed to enjoy bringing all his strength and youth to such jobs; the duller the people, the more he wolfed them down and found special qualities in them. He would investigate grey areas of England, mud puddles stocked with good people, and walk about eagerly, looking at everything with brilliant, interested eyes. During the week, he was at the Treasury, and so kennelled up that after that anything became sport. But the contrast with his father was so extraordinary, it must have been deliberate. Rudi had a very large and very well-known Elizabethan manor house in the country, and let the public in during the season. In spite of the outhouses and stables, the formal and kitchen gardens, the animals, etc., he couldn't bear a single grey day there, and would jump into the car and drive straight back to London, terrified, if he found himself alone and it began to rain.

I wasn't a traveller, and never wanted to go away, even with Philip. And I had to do everything *so well*. I must present a casual, swinging appearance, wearing the very latest clothes and make-up. That was all part of his smartness—not exactly his physical smartness—I had to represent his *mental* smartness, and thus allow him to dress carelessly, really rather badly. He was quite handsome enough for this, and as he was always in a hurry, due to a well-planned life, he gave the appearance of a young godlike Londoner, with the round, stern face of Hermes, flying along the pavements in a badly cut suit with a purse of the people's money in his hand. But let someone not his equal try to get into conversation with this protector of the people! Then it really was the stone face of a god which met them as they obstructed his path. Philip believed in power, and in himself. Other people were influences on *him*.

All this had a solidarity to it which no sensible woman was going to reject. But, even more overwhelming, there was something I used—almost—to forget between meetings. And that was his extreme physical attractiveness, his healthy indoor skin with moonlight behind it, let alone the glowing eyes and thick hair—this kept the relationship fresh, brand-new, because it always took me by surprise, and made me try harder each time. So the chase was still on, every day, worse than ever. And we were so close, so settled, that I was invited to delude myself and had to wake myself up and tear the scales from my eyes, as if inside a dream, drowsy and intoxicating, which *must* be controlled.

The strain was very great. Philip was the sort of man with whose life nothing could possibly go wrong; decisions were permanent, and ended at death.

There was no horse-hair coachwork in Philip's club—just pools of light, écritoires, and groups of clean chintz chairs on heavy pile carpet.

He was sitting at a desk, putting the stamps on some letters when I arrived.

"Darling ..."

He got up, overjoyed, and kissed my cheek. I realised that I was three-quarters of an hour late, and he said not a word. By the letters was a whisky and soda which looked as though it had been sipped only. I was always impressed by men with careful habits, and relieved that I was lucky enough to have one.

"Oh you look marvellous!"

"Do I? I'm all glued together."

"I love it. I love the eyelashes."

"Oh bother. Can you see them?"

"You don't think that by this time I don't know what your eyes look like, do you?"

"I always think I'm deceiving people."

We sat comfortably in the club, looking doltishly into one another's eyes. Philip was so *fit.* His warm well-fed body beside me, with its bills paid up and feet laced into well-fitting shoes, was the most desirable living thing in London. Philip had the ability to put a dark gleam—a piece of reckless erotic mischief-making—into his eyes: "Look at what I'm thinking about—see that? Huh! I don't mince words in here, I can tell you!" At such moments he was always conquered by his own innocent wickedness, and would begin to laugh in hopeless carnal guffaws when my expression told him that he'd been found out, and no one was in the least bit shocked. But he also had a clock buried in his flesh, and said now:

"I think we'd better have dinner soon ..."

That meant straight away. We went slowly and formally up the great staircase to the club dining-room. Philip walked in the middle of the stairs, bisecting the rest of the traffic.

Each table had flowers and a silver candelabrum. All the women sat carefully and talked in modulated voices; on the whole they were rather bony women but so charming and well-informed that the atmosphere invigorated you in spite of the bone-yard feeling. Philip filled in what looked like a bill foil; he would sign it at the end of the meal.

"Cauliflower?"

We had to get every detail of the meal right. And I mustn't make jokes; this instantly made a cauliflower exceedingly funny.

"Yes please." I choked down the idiot glee.

"What's so funny?"

"Nothing ... the people's vegetable." I knew that was provocative, and could be taken as a jibe, since he was so left wing. Heaven knows why I said it. Perhaps because I found his socialism so snobbish, so exclusive, so bogus.

He decided to let it go, but looked disapproving.

"Potatoes?" He said it in such a potatoey voice that I choked again.

"What *is* the matter with you this evening?"

"Nothing." I suddenly had a feeling I wouldn't do for him. "It's just ... all these vegetables."

"You don't have to have any vegetables at all if you don't want them," he said rather shortly, and closed the menu.

We sat in a serious silence considering the problem of vegetables. What had got into me? I always looked forward to the meals at his club, which were really the only proper meals I had, especially with those big grey potatoes. Philip blew his nose in a way that showed he felt left out and wanted attention.

"Have you got a cold?" I asked with sudden liveliness.

"Yes." He was sorry for himself.

"Oh my God!" I moved away from him involuntarily.

"Come on, Sophie, you're a very healthy woman. One little cold isn't going to kill you."

"Oh Lord."

"*I've* had it all the week."

"And now you're going to give it to me." The curious fact is that at the same time I was thinking: "I shall never love anyone as I love Philip."

He seemed to have been listening to my thoughts, because quite suddenly he smiled at me with great sweetness. Too late! You're done for! You'll never get away from a man who smiles at you like that.

We were well into the meal by this time, and I was just putting out the blade of my knife to cut my piece of cauliflower, when I saw an unmistakable caterpillar, a huge white one, which had been cooked *whole*. It was very much like a piece of cauliflower, and was lying on its back covered with white sauce. With all these new false eyelashes to cope with, I should never have noticed it but for the feet—I don't know how many pairs—but they all had black boots on. I looked privately towards Philip, wondering whether I dared mention it. Because it was a slight on *his* cauliflower, at *his* club. It was almost as though I'd deliberately planted it there, in order to be objectionable: "Here's the people's vegetable and here's one of the people in it," played to the old nursery rhyme jingle of "Here's the church and here's the steeple, Open the doors and here are the people."

I knew he'd felt that indecisive glance in his direction. He looked at me with the clear-gazing steadiness of Englishmen—a mannerism he used when exposing the weakness in someone else's argument on television. I decided to eat the caterpillar and die; or perhaps to eat around it. Then Philip saw it for himself and, at once, it became an incident. With his arm raised to exactly the right level, to indicate he was intercepting the waiter for something serious, he held his displeasure in dumb-show, in limbo, until one of them arrived hot-foot at the barrier of the arm. Then the confidential aside. Meanwhile I presided over the upturned boots, trying not to take too much interest in them, until both Philip and the waiter gazed at them with perfectly blank faces, as if looking at something Byzantine in a cabinet in the Victoria and Albert Museum. They were taken away. No one smiled. Philip apologised to me as if I were a colleague in the Treasury. I brushed it off. We went on eating and drinking like two silly marionettes in a vaudeville act entitled "At Dinner." I suddenly began to miss—of all people—my mother. Why couldn't I turn to Philip and say in a loaded voice: "Did you see its *boots*?" Because I knew he would reply: "Don't go on about a trivial matter." Philip knew what life was all about and was so grown-up that this should have helped me to bring myself up to the same level. Instead of which I seemed to be trying to have my childhood over again with him, or, what was worse, my boyhood, because my mother had taken mine away from me.

Or, was it perhaps the strain of our relationship which made me behave in this way? Yes, I suddenly understood. I had a grudge against him because he kept me dangling. I was tired of gluing on false eyelashes, and wanted *reality*. If there was to be no reality, then I was entitled to play and exasperate him.

I finished my wine, and said cheerfully:

"Boots."

For this I got a slight smile that vanished instantly in his cheek. The shutters were down. And ten minutes later we were in the car.

Driving off into the night always pleased Philip. He felt he was stealing a march on other ambitious young men. I had wound a long fox-tail around my neck. I smoked, and looked out over the top of it with a not-too-agreeable expression. He gave me a very approving nod; just right; sulking too, perfect.

This made me frown again. How many more nights? How many more fox furs?

He snapped certain gadgets on and off. There was no peace until the car had been heated, tuned, adjusted. I lit another cigarette and again got through it in silence. It began to rain. The windscreen-wipers were noisy; they set up a rhythm, with the rubber welts uttering moans as they drew arches on the glass. The rain increased. There was a familiar teeming-down sound from overhead which woke prehistoric memories of crouching safely undercover while the waters, in sweetened glistening drops, raced by just clear of your face. It allowed you to rest for an instant, break off the chase, and take some contentment purely on your own account. The humidity brought out the smell of fox in my fur.

As the wipers went on mumbling, they groaned especially loudly every now and then when they pressed themselves too close to the glass.

"It's somewhere here." Philip was looking for the hotel.

"Ancient or modern?"

"Modern. A high block. We should be able to see it."

"Noisy windscreen-wipers."

Silence. And so I said:

"Can you hear what they're saying?"

"No."

"'*Oh the brethren, Oh the brethren.*'"

Philip was turning his head this way and that. As soon as the phrase "*Oh the brethren*" was out of my mouth, I realised how fatally accurate it was. From that moment you couldn't hear anything else. The rain seethed around us and the windscreen-wipers repeated solemnly: "*Oh the brethren, Oh the brethren, Oh the brethren.*"

Very irritated, he switched them off.

"Look here, Sophie, if you're doing this to annoy me this evening …"

In the middle of what should have been laughter, I was dumb with sorrow and shook my head.

We sat there behind the flowing, swilling windscreen. Then he tried the wipers again cautiously. "*Oh the brethren!*" cried the wipers loudly and fervently. He clicked them off, and stuck his head out of the window.

"Oh. I see it."

"Oh thank God."

"Now we'll just … grit our teeth … and go … like mad."

We lurched and then accelerated dangerously down a pitch-dark curving drive lined with laurel bushes which swamped us as we struck them. "*Oh the brethren, Oh the brethren*" chanted the wipers faster than ever, trying to keep up with us. And making an effort to break the mantra which was driving us insane, I shouted against it:

"You see, I suppose I was thinking of a sort of Masonic evening—with old men—and by accident—I hit it off too well—I'm so sorry."

"*Ther-bre-ther-rennnn,*" going into a nasal drone as we slowed down and finally stopped. I was huddled up in my seat like a miserable clammy frog with bolting eyes, asking to be forgiven. What for? For—making life funny.

Philip took his hands off the wheel, and turned and kissed me on the brow, which meant: "Don't do that again, and we'll say no more about it." His young face, with raindrops on it, kissing me naturally and being cool like a child's face, touched me.

"I've got a cold," he said childishly, finding another excuse for himself.

"Yes, darling. It's horrid. I'll put you to bed." Soothing words like that flowed out of my mouth without me really hearing them. We got out, united.

4

A new hotel bedroom, a new playground, always went to my head like alcohol. Even before touching one another we ran about the room together, smiling and in high spirits, possessing it. You pulled a cord to light the bathroom, which was a brilliant Aladdin's cave with blue scooped-out bath and blue tiles with some shimmering crusts of stone in them. The bath had a glassy curtain, taps like nuggets of platinum, moulded by being held in an enormous hot hand, two miniature blue soaps (male and female) and towels as thick as ploughed fields under snow. The bedroom was too hot and the window, with steel edges and no window-sill, wouldn't open. By pressing my face against the glass, I could see the forty-foot drop outside.

Philip was playing with the wooden headboard which stretched half way down the room and had many knobs in it. He rang the metal waste-paper basket with his foot.

"Where's the fire escape?" I asked.

"Round the back somewhere."

I went down the corridor to look for it. There wasn't one. We were all sealed in forty foot above ground with no way of escape. I found some stairs, and calculated whether I could get down them in time, and decided that that was where the flames would come up. The lift was a tightly closed metal box suitable for weakening the resistance of normal human beings in order that they should confess to things they hadn't done. Once inside you lost all sense of yourself, gravity, good and evil. If the light went out you committed suicide as quietly as you could.

In spite of my hotel bedroom euphoria, my instinct for self-preservation was alerted. Eventually, after roaming down more sealed corridors, I saw through a window that it might be possible to jump across to the roof of the kitchen block of the hotel by going down to the floor below and breaking the glass of another so-called window.

With this gloomy satisfaction in hand, I returned slowly to the bedroom ... Yes, the bedroom, which should have been the safe, welcoming erotic centre of the night, was turning into a trap in which we washed ourselves with blue soap and were grilled at dawn while escaping to the kitchen block.

I burst into the room, to find Philip scarlet from the heat, and said wildly:

"Oh why can't we go to an old-fashioned hotel with cream paint, turkey carpets and warming pans ... near *the ground*?"

"Poor darling." Philip put his arms around me. He was perfectly happy in these surroundings, and was literally smiling from ear to ear, what with the gadgets, television, air-conditioning, central heating, give-away bubble bath, forms to be filled in for breakfast and different notices to be hung on the door.

"It's too much," I said feebly.

"Poor little darling, come to bed," he began thoughtfully undressing me, and kept me quiet by stroking me at the same time.

"It won't do ..."

"We'll never come here again."

I abused him softly, but my tiredness was, by then, on the point of exploding me. How I underestimated myself!

Inside that kind of tiredness is a fierce uninhibited strength, which you cannot obtain from yourself when calm and healthy. You need a dirty, bad-tempered face, a sensation of wretchedness and uncertainty about the future which makes you demand everything from the present. Was the hotel built with that in view?

I dropped all my cares, and it appeared that we were already half naked without apparently having undressed. There was no time for that. We had set up camp hastily on the end of the bed where his lecture-notes and my fox-tail couldn't be got rid of for the moment. We did not stop to breathe, think, turn aside for an instant, but drove on in the way we had begun. Each time this happened between us I beheld him with amazement. It was the appalling strength and kindness of the drive that frightened me; we had to hold hands like children now and again, palm to palm, to comfort and reassure one another in case a moment of loneliness had set in, due to too much desire acted out with open eyes, so that one of us might have become deeply afraid. How intelligent we were! We wanted to please one another, partly because we owed it to ourselves. There was only one thing we could not do. We could not stop. How terrifying that was.

We *thought* we were in control. But if he had turned away from me at that moment, I would have struck him, and become almost ugly and venomous with my demands, who ten minutes ago merely wanted to go home! As it was, if he dared to pause for an instant—an instant that was not pleasing to me—I would re-light him with a peremptory glance more rapid than a blink. And the responsibility for this behaviour was not mine, but *ours*. We exchanged sexes, following and leading alternately, and watching one another as sharply as hunters, as we woke one another up.

I got from my tiredness this pitiless behaviour and gave it to him, because that was what I knew he wanted *and that was what he drew out of me* ... In the middle of it, he smiled openly at me with real love—it was unbearable. I put my face away to the side, swamped with self-pity.

"There is no one like him, no one."

"What, my darling?"

"Nothing."

Philip said: "I love you so much."

These words and tiredness, the drunkenness that makes you too drunk to stop drinking, had lowered my resistance to life, and made me afraid of losing him. At once, I wanted to stop and regain my detachment. I wanted my own thoughts back again; in the circumstances, he had no right to take them away from me and make over my psyche, binding it with love, only to return me, exhausted and broken, to my own life. My look also said: "And you have no right to smile like that with your whole soul—like a worshipping, adoring angel—you *animal*."

He read my face correctly. And since his love for me had no fear or resentment in it (unlike my own) he drew enough pure anger for himself from my expression to raise the carnal level between us to the totality he so much wanted. I understood him instantly, loved him, and held him: the gods stopped the fight inside me. I was so sorry for everything.

When we made friends again, inside the old friendship, we were lying side by side, two clean, healthy bodies clasped softly together, our hands weak brooches or the clasps on old books that are coming undone ... having made such strange love, so young, but so full of regrets, so homeless ... that we might not have done if we had been securely married to one another for the last two years.

I was able to see my situation again. And moving off to a certain distance in my thoughts, I was able to say to myself as before: "Besides you're far too handsome. This muscular, sweet-smelling creature to be given to me? What a feast! No, it's too much." I poured as much enamel as was needed for my sophistication and recovery.

I found my head to be lying, as if it had been there a century, jammed into a piece of crumpled typescript like a coconut wrapped for a shy. My bones hadn't enough marrow in them to allow me to move for the moment, and gravity had doubled my weight so that I was sunk into the hotel eiderdown as if into a sandpit. Getting there had been so tiring that the physical weariness was like a battle with the sea. There was the same physical *shock*, after which you remained "dead," slumped in the same recumbent posture on the beach ... and if a dog should come up to you and lick you, or even bark at you, or if the foam on the edge of a long wave should touch your foot, you would not move a muscle, but go on and on and on, lying there, perfectly happy ... triumphant, in fact, with a feeling of achievement ... overjoyed by every additional second of life ...

At this moment of absolute stillness, both inside myself and outside in the room, I suddenly thought of Princess Melika's Blue Poppy. But that was from another world! An old-fashioned world, full of furniture. Whereas Philip's world was modern and all the objects in it seemed to be brand-new. But although I appeared to be going forward in this world, which was also mine by generation, all I was actually doing was changing rooms to make love in. Those ingredients for life which Melika had were the things which were lacking in our world: there were no additional dimensions, above all, no fun. Everything Philip said and did was deadly serious. Blue poppies might be ludicrous, out of date, but what was to replace them? Even *with* Philip I was living inside a hole. He didn't believe in the invisible world; and it was obvious to me that I was getting ill without it.

I lay there. Making love weakens you, and you badly need something firm (or of illusory firmness) to grasp afterwards. It was in my nature to look for something more. And Philip would only say: "There isn't anything more." But my mother, and Pussy Melika, and his own father, Rudolf Horner ... and especially Guy ... all had in their lives a kind of spiritual vitality. My mother always had on a spiritual drama, a battle for her own soul, as a matter of daily existence. Her world was younger than Philip's world. And when I was away from him, on my own, the world smelled younger than it did right now.

From the moment I was with him, I was physically mesmerised and took up his attitudes. Even the people in the street changed completely; they became all one class, slightly dowdy, but solid, worthy and hard-working. I was always seeing nurses when I was with Philip, or intellectual young men striding fast and pale with study. When we were in the parks, we passed whole families soberly walking out together, taking the air, whereas when I was alone I was always passing laughing girls, in dashing purple clothes, whisperers, parasites.

Wherever we went, Philip was always in command, responsible for everything. I had never been so much at the centre of society, ready to give my name and address and my views on the latest news at a moment's notice. Life with Philip meant lectures, concerts, club dinners, theatres, cinemas, small parties, hard work, a firm mind, and non-stop love-making.

And this—to me—unbearably ordinary world of his was made not only bearable, but magical, on account of his beauty and energy. I was so proud of him. But his way of life was emphatically a *man's* way of life; it was too male for me. And it was wearing me out.

I knew that he was fighting the image of his father; the trouble was that he was succeeding in a way that was changing *me*. Philip never spoke of his father; he disapproved of him, and he would have disapproved of my mother too, but for the fact that he had known her for years and was used to her. I always prayed she wouldn't let me down when he was there; and she always did. If only by siding with him, flirtatiously, because he represented authority. She had no status, no *cause*, no bosom, no money; she was just a mother. And I was just a daughter. And I didn't think it was going to be enough.

So Philip was changing me, unknown to him. I could feel myself changing *at that very minute*. I was becoming more secretive but more self-reliant, less affectionate (in case he thought I was asking for something) but more efficient at getting things done.

I understood very well that with a father twice divorced Philip was highly nervous about marriage. He thought his father was immoral on every level of his existence. No wonder Philip wanted to grasp the essentials of an orderly life and had no intention of making a mistake. I felt I was a mistake right then as I lay on his lecture notes. And when I was among his friends it was a hundred times worse.

I was really terrified of the women in Philip's set. They were all male women, capable adults with two or three babies each and opinions on everything. Name any subject, and they had a brand-new set of opinions on it. Another thing: I hadn't had a miscarriage or an abortion, and that marked me down straight away. I was the odd one out. I couldn't talk about pregnancy; didn't even want to. My own illnesses, which had been terrible and ignominious, were unconnected with sex, so I knew they were irrelevant and must not be mentioned. I also knew I was getting myself hated with every day that passed when I still had no miscarriage to talk about. No left wing and no miscarriage? It was appalling. You cannot hope to become a fertility tyrant of the middle classes, and earn the right to exclude, snub and humble others, without a story about babies (your own, of course. Talking about other people's babies isn't selfish enough. Therefore it's unnatural.) I wanted that baby very much indeed, but I didn't want to talk about it.

What was even worse was that I sometimes talked about Mr Ruback's teaching, mysticism ... and would, in the future, speak of the blue poppy. On these occasions I was immediately treated as a little girl. They knew what was going on; a danger to their cause—something difficult that ran against the grain of natural, mechanical life, something childish, lonely, awkward, and dangerous, if not outright comic, they knew what that was: escapism.

It was those damn dark blue regulation knickers all over again.

I was suddenly exceptionally tired of having to justify myself. Tired of being judged by standards which were heartless and narrow, and which I didn't believe in. Tired of hearing the word "bitch" and trying to engross it normally into my conversation. "What's the use?" came over me and flooded out everything else. It all became too much, and I lost heart. The great structure of this love of mine, with its underpinning of admiration, regularity, honesty, courtesy, simply collapsed into a flat heap.

At that moment when I thought Philip to be fast asleep, centrally heated to boiling point, he lifted up his head and looked at me happily.

I hadn't time to change my expression, couldn't get a smile across my face quickly enough, but stared at him for an instant with my whole mind, so terribly sad, the whole sub-continent of two years' expectation and heartsick disappointment there to be seen.

"What is it? What is it? Don't look at me like that!"

That look of mine was so resigned, it was in the nature of a decision. He held on to me anxiously, kissed my face, made a cradle of his arms and rocked me as though he could lull the storm in that way. In between he would look quickly into my eyes to see how things were. I repaired the idiotic give-away instantly, put something fresh in the window and said politely:

"Quite all right."

"What's quite all right? Please tell me."

"Really there's nothing to tell you. Truthfully."

"Oh there must be. For you to look like that."

"Nonsense. Just overtired. You know how tired I get."

"Sophie." He stopped the words by speaking my name to me with intense tenderness. "What is it *really*?" begging me with his large, brilliant eyes, not to tell him what it was *really*.

I have always loathed deliberate hypocrisy; it makes me physically ill and forces me to speak the truth. If he had said nothing at that moment, I should have said nothing. I'd been careless with my thoughts—leaving them out where they could be seen. I acknowledged it. And I was prepared to be talked round and not to make a fuss. That was part of the game. But hypocrisy was not; Philip was so used to facing up to things that he thought he owed it to *us* to do so now. Unfortunately facing up to things and *pretending* to face up to them are rather different. The result was that he amused me; and I looked at him shrewdly, feeling much lighter already. At this moment I could say more or less anything with a dash of truth in it. So I said:

"I don't think you know what you want."

He replied at dictation speed with a great deal of care, in fact far too much:

"I want you."

The curious fact was that he meant it, but someone coming into the cinema at that moment could be well and truly forgiven for thinking the reverse. I nearly said: "Oh please, do that bit again, a little better."

And aware that he had spoken badly and was forcing himself out onto dangerous ground (quite unnecessarily, because I had turned my head away when he said that, in order not to embarrass him), he suddenly got up and began to walk to and fro on it, testing every inch. Obviously danger was what he needed at the moment.

We had both forgotten we were naked. Philip had been half-covered by a bedcover, which slid off his white thigh as he rose.

I made an enfeebled movement towards some blue satin pyjamas from Biba's which were up on the pillow. I dragged them over me; they slithered about and were icy. Ugh: nothing brings you to your senses more quickly.

Philip was pacing out a measure in a way he did when giving a lecture, swayed by gusts of politics, or possessing the fireplace at his club. Being well-covered, he was always at ease without his clothes; one of the reasons why he was often so badly dressed. His highly sexed body, now totally unconnected with sex, roamed to and fro. As soon as he got lost among his thoughts, he imagined he *was* dressed. He was going to force himself to speak at any moment now, and the timing was wrong, the hot-house setting disastrous. If a fresh wind had blown in on us, we would have lifted our heads, caught one another's expressions and gone quietly to bed. I felt like giving him half of my stone-cold pyjamas and saying: "Here, try this on. You'll feel much better afterwards."

No, he wanted to drag overheated, dramatic words out of his naked body. And coming up to me, he braced himself and began to broadcast a message just to one side of my head, as experienced speakers will direct their voices just to one side of a microphone. It went slowly, in neutral tones, and seemed as important as the famous Declaration of War broadcast by the BBC. I felt his breath.

"I was going to ask you to come and live with me. But I can't promise you there won't be an emotional bust-up in five years' time. And then you'll be less well off financially than you are now."

Oh Philip, my great love.

I wanted to block up my ears in case there was anything more to come; these ears which could not believe what they were hearing. In fact I did cover my face with my hands, because no matter what people say, words can break bones. The message seemed to drip into my ears like poison, and to go on dripping in afterwards, like the black death. I shall never forget it as long as I live. It was so unexpected that I couldn't really hear it; I went on listening, re-playing it and re-shuffling the words until they made sense ... and then disbelieving the sense. It was so much worse than anything I could have imagined.

I kept my face covered, and he moved off. Then I heard him in the bathroom. The blue bathroom, the Aladdin's cabin with the snow-deep towels and blue soaps—but that was on the other side of eternity now.

I rose up quietly, with dry, burnt eyes, put my pyjamas on and got into one side of the bed. It was a double bed and I regretted it. I switched out the light on my side, and lay absolutely still, like a wrapped-up frozen piece of meat.

Philip returned, and had remembered to bring himself a glass of water because I heard him put it down. He sat on his side of the bed for a moment. Then he said, apparently to himself:

"Well, goodnight then."

He switched out the light. And healing, liberating darkness covered us. How sweet that darkness was. I had been waiting for it and I wanted to fold myself into the very centre of it. It was then that I realised I was trembling without control from delayed shock, and I began to have great difficulty with my breathing. It was being controlled by my heart, which had just been broken, and was retaliating by tightly constricting my chest with some iron bands. I couldn't get the air into my lungs, exactly as though I had asthma.

I knew these emotional symptoms would give me away to my enemy, who lay so close to me. I slid myself out of the side of the bed and, groping about in the deep darkness, I found the eiderdown. I, who was so afraid of the dark and slept every night with a night-light, was now safer a hundred times inside it, free to tremble as I chose. And so, wrapped in the eiderdown, lying on the floor, I trembled. And lying not far away on the bed was the unforgiving man who had been my lover.

I was not going to be forgiven by this man for hasty, flamboyant words, or for pieces of extravagant behaviour from the past. His love had not been an uncritical love. Pussy Melika loved me with that kind of love and I knew the difference now. Inside her love I could behave badly, just as Guy did, and she would not turn away from me, but would wait until I found myself again. Philip had hardened his heart against me in the same way that I hardened my heart against my mother, in case she should become a nuisance in a busy life. In fact, in trying to please him I had become unnatural to her, hoping that we could both pass in his eyes as well-balanced citizens, in that strong puritan classless class I saw abroad in his modern world. I now realised how absurd this was. I wept to think I should ever have pressed her to conform, when the qualities she brought to life were unique, dazzling, wholly irrelevant to that society, being well outside its range. I had taken her way of life for granted; the gentle sensibility (so easily hurt), the jokes that so improved life, the amusing friends, the deep humanity, the ability to play, believe, dream and forgive.

And here I was on the floor in the dark, unmistakably repudiated by the modern world, thrown out to eat the air. I hadn't deceived any of them, not for one minute. Oh the coarseness of his evaluation of life, himself and myself in pounds and pence and the exact time-limit set for the relationship to run! These were the things that paralysed my mind. As though one could actually stop loving someone on a certain date; stop eating partridge, say, at the age of forty-four, when the alarm clock went off, and start on quail. His estimate of his appetite for me was extremely practical.

That was how he was. A plain-speaking man. And because he had just been honest, he had earned his sleep, which he was now taking with his strong limbs comfortably stretched out in bed.

Didn't you say to yourself half an hour ago that even with Philip you were living inside a hole? Now you're without him and how slowly the minutes pass. You won't have to look past his shoulder for anything more now, because you're alone. If there's a hole, it's your hole; and all you have to do is to fill it. Do you think you'll be able to do that?

At first the loneliness down there on the floor was so excruciating that at every second I thought I should have to call out: "Help!" With the trembling and the panic came nausea; I was mad for some words of comfort and I understood now why old people talk to themselves and soldiers sing when they are afraid. It stops the bile rising and deludes the stomach so that the heaving dies down. Even children chatter themselves to sleep when they are alone.

And so I treated myself like a child down there, and asked myself in a whisper what it was I wanted at that moment. "Air" came the reply so promptly that I almost laughed. There wasn't anything wrong with a subconscious as wide awake as that.

I was astounded to think now that I had been lying there tamely, letting Philip destroy me minute by minute. If I had listened to my subconscious a little earlier, I could have revived myself with a drink of oxygen long ago. A drink of the night air which was flowing by outside; pure, inky, refreshing, at forty foot up. It would surely be as strong as Pussy's vodka after all that rain which had washed out the sky from top to bottom, and had been thrown across the sky from one side to another, as music is thrown across a concert hall and washes up into the corners.

I picked myself up and felt my way across the black box of a room, being intercepted by one of those wooden chairs which stick out like crutches and are set at an angle across a corner to prevent you getting at the window. When I pulled aside the thick frock-coats of the curtains, I saw the day of a blue night. Oh what a good sight for a trembling woman, wrapped in an eiderdown. I settled down to the business of cracking the window. After I had gone over it very carefully, I found a three-quarter inch ledge of warm metal running along the bottom. I tried with all my strength to raise it, and to my amazement it moved, and in a moment or two I had an opening of about eight inches. Through those eight inches came the living silence of the English countryside and the breath of heaven, just as I had wanted them. I was re-united with natural forces, and in a few seconds I stopped trembling, and began to breathe regularly and repair myself. The thirstiness passed off; my face was washed by the passing breeze, I have never tasted anything like it. Through that gap in the plating of the hotel, I began to carry on my life once again. I was like a grateful, convalescent dog, that sobs and whimpers, and nearly swoons away with dog-like sentimentality for the gift of the mist and the night air.

After a few minutes I looked back into the stupefying darkness, where there was a stranger lying fast asleep. How on earth had I come to know him? Oh yes: through our families, of whom he disapproved. Through his father, who was liked by everyone, and who made one mistake after another; who existed, solely and uniquely, to "make trouble." And who had married, years and years ago, an unknown woman with a yellow velvet sofa. My God, what kind of a woman was she, who had built so much good sense, so much cold potato, into the head of her son? I saw a first-class mind embedded in a highly edible first-class English potato ... sitting-up *properly* on a sofa, as if she was going to play the piano ... "Father won't leave me a penny, you know," Philip once said to me sharply. "Really?" "No. He doesn't like me. He'll leave it all to Guy." "But you don't believe in property?" "No. But one has to live decently." He said it while standing in the middle of my flat, looking critically at the new curtains I had just hung. So, in spite of himself, he was after all, the true child of the yellow sofa.

Perhaps his memo-writing at the Treasury was only a phase in his development. In that case he would not be able to be himself until his father was dead; he could then stop reacting against him. His modern flat in Wimpole Street with the aluminium lampshades, and his bedside book *Steering the Economy* with graphs and calendars of events in it, would all go up in smoke; the alarm clock would go off; he would start on quail. But at this moment his whole way of life was held together by a fertile distaste for his father.

No, it was *I* who had gone in the wrong direction. I must re-trace my steps and start again. It was *I* who had made the mistake. Oh dear, why will people make speeches late at night in which they say things that they mean?

"Go to sleep, Sophie." It was my mother's voice from the young old-fashioned world of Hampstead. I went obediently back into the gloom, decided that I had earned my share of the bed, but that I would keep the eiderdown as a barrier. As I got into bed, the sleeper made a movement towards me, but I turned him over by the shoulder like an efficient nurse, without waking him. I remembered that I hadn't washed: I hated going to bed unwashed and uncombed, but I knew that I must try to sleep while my morale was reasonable. I mustn't risk falling apart all alone in the blue bathroom, which had been such a brilliant water toy with its boat of a bath, for two carefree people. I resigned myself to my snoring, comatose bedfellow, and pulled the blankets up over my head. So this was a night with the beloved …

In the morning, everything would appear to be in order again. We wouldn't refer to what had happened. Philip would probably wake me, smiling at me, with a breakfast menu to be filled in, asking:

"Bacon and eggs?" Cauliflower? Quail?

5

It took me days to throw that hotel bedroom prison scene out of my mind. It was always replaying itself, with lights and dialogue, in some corner of my head, while I was cleaning out the flat, writing letters, picking the newspaper off the mat in the morning. Right up in a penthouse at the top of the lift-shaft in my brain, that scene was taking place. Independence is a letter-box of your own that makes a good noise when the postman comes, but it also means living with these television sets carelessly left on inside your head, and broadcasting the wrong sort of news. In fact it wasn't until the night of the lecture that I'd built a mound of ordinary life in there, strong enough to keep it out and stop the wasteful nonsense. And I was tired of going back and sitting in on certain scenes in order to re-do my hair or go over my mouth with a scarlet gloss lipstick because the central heating had given my lips a dry puckered skin, a sad mouth of baked mud that looked as though it had left behind forever the art of kissing.

The poison we made together in that room was so vile that I came out in boils on my chin and beside my nose. My mother seemed in a curious way to be pleased, as though it made her more attractive that I should be less attractive. She knew instinctively that I had had some agonising blow. Philip took back two books by H.G. Wells he had borrowed from her, and stopped there for tea. They got on like a house on fire; my mother always sided with male authority. She phoned me up afterwards, still laughing. She even patronised me slightly, and told me certain things about the ways of men which I didn't at all want to hear. She said: "I don't like to hear you like this," because for one split second I was careless, and couldn't keep the sob out of my voice. She also said: "I don't like to think of you being the suppliant," and rang off in good spirits.

That unfortunate word "suppliant" nearly took me round to her cottage with a bomb. It makes me bridle even now; she smacked her lips over it when she said it, as though she'd just dipped into the Bible, was on very good terms with God, and needed a good sharp pinch to make her human again.

On the night of the lecture she phoned and asked me: "You're not in the clutches of that drug-taker, are you?"

"What drug-taker?"

"You know the man I mean."

"I certainly don't."

"A certain Mr Ruback."

There was a heavy, important pause. She waited for me to say something that would implicate me. She was at her naughtiest, straight out of some intrigue in Vb form room with Biddy Horner. These were the moments when I knew I had brought her up badly and spoilt her by kissing her too often.

"You mean the poor man we saw in the street the other day? And you said he had a nice, clean neck, just like my father's."

"If your father were alive he would have stepped in long ago, and stopped all this nonsense."

"That's not you. That's Biddy Horner."

"Naturally we want to know what you're up to. Is it L.S.D.?"

It was almost worth having this conversation to hear my mother say "L.S.D." in practice tones and with a little cough, as she always did when trying to bring her vocabulary up to date. In gruff butcher boy's voice I growled:

"Yer mean the acid, huh?"

She *hated* being teased. Just like Philip when I said: "You haven't said '*sine qua non*' for eight weeks. I don't like it." But I thought she was being frivolous about something serious. I suppose it was true that "the man up the road," Mr Ruback, who lectured at the top of Christchurch Hill, was forming and moulding and changing Guy and myself into different people. My mother said:

"Why can't you come to church with me like a normal daughter?"

"Because I can't stand the boredom."

"And are these lectures so—so exciting?"

"Yes."

For a moment I thought she was going to say "How can they be?" as though the great subjects of life (i.e. life itself), death, cause and effect, energy, morality and purpose had always been so dull for her on account of the intoned platitudes of church services which filled the mind with fog and wool, that she bitterly resented the cocktail party I was going to. The fact that I regarded the lectures as "a good time" was quite enough evidence that they were polluted, immoral. How can answers to great, imponderable mysteries be regarded as "a good time"? Where was the suffering? Everyone knows that you're here to suffer.

But the main thing was, she didn't want to understand because it was *strange*. But is there anything stranger than going to an Anglican church? And her questions were not really questions, any more than interviewers' questions are when they talk to well-known people. That kind of question is a peck from a beak which would like to peck you to death. While they are pecking you, you begin to lose all interest in yourself, and you become like a hunted animal—wild, desperate. Then they can turn on you in triumph and say you're aggressive: "Don't be so aggressive about everything!" "But I wasn't aggressive before you attacked me." "There you go again! Who's attacking you?" Peck, peck, peck.

No wonder Guy had such a highly developed persecution complex, and my own was coming on quite well too today. But his mother, Biddy, was a pecker of the very first rank. In addition to the words, she was a *silent* pecker; and anyone who's been pecked away in silence will know what that means. Guy didn't give her his address when he got himself a room on the Île St Louis, and she had to send the pecking letters to a Poste Restante address on the right bank. Then, on the days when he felt strong enough, he would take the right bank, the sober bank, and walk to the post office at the Hotel de Ville, and queue up, and receive her letters into his hand, which instantly began to tremble. He would walk about with the envelopes intact for some time and then, sitting down beside the Seine, looking about him at the vistas—at the lower part of the banks which have stone boulevards where people are silently fishing or thinking watery thoughts while the trees, far away up above, planted with their roots in the high traffic boulevard that roars, cover all the levels with water-green leaves—looking about him he would be reassured and carelessly open the letters, and after half an hour he would go off dull, leaden, anxious, guilty.

My mother was not really a pecker. She was too young in spirit and had to learn it from Biddy. And she was bad at it. For example, with a movement of sympathy, she finished this conversation by saying:

"Oh well, if it means something to you."

It meant everything to me.

On lecture nights, Guy and I would walk up the long hill together, talking as hard and fast as I should have been able to talk to Philip. Another thing. Guy had a face that moved about in a human way; whereas Philip had developed the poker face of the self-made man, who doesn't want to get too intimate with you, doesn't want too many of your thoughts, even while making passionate love to you ... men who do not really want to live with a woman, cannot comprehend what it means to bury yourself in someone else's thoughts and in their physical presence, and only to feel really well and complete there ...

It was dusk. I spent ten minutes cutting the mud of Hampstead Heath out of my boots. It was very satisfying to get a shape from the instep in a wedge like chocolate. I loved the smell of the black polish, as healthy as ozone. I suppose I connected it with the feeling of well-being the lectures gave me. I noticed that Mr Ruback's black shoes were always polished, and his face gave out calm good health—the shiny bits might even have been rubbed up with a soft cloth. Guy and I had been introduced to the lecture group by a friend of Guy's, a silent boy with a white face who worked in a post office. Each of us went for our own reasons; mine was a desire for hard information on invisible forces inside and outside myself. I wanted to know why I questioned everything: and everyone else did not. Although I found the lectures through Guy, I didn't absorb the teaching through his sensibility. On the contrary, I took what I needed for myself; in my efforts to find out about myself and the universe I lived in I was single-minded and ignored him ... until I found out that he was equally single-minded and was getting along as fast or faster than I was.

From that moment we began to talk out to one another. On the evenings when I walked to the lectures with him, everything had the safety and permanence of objects in my childhood. The world had violin-cases (in which blocks of amber rosin knocked about) and fishing-rods in it again. And the people at the lectures were *real* people, not inhuman grey mushrooms who kept talking about "efficiency" and spoke not a word when you were alone with them. It was one of the few places where you saw real people today, talkative, friendly, polite, contented, amusing—it wouldn't have done for Philip at all. It occurred to me that the visitors from outer space were already here, filling up the streets, appearing on T.V., standing up in Parliament to make speeches, interrogating one another about their opinions, all conforming, marrying, making mushroom children, and passing themselves off as human beings. Mushrooms, marionettes, dogs.

But those of us who went to the lectures had a secret, a rendez-vous, an idea. It was like sneaking off to hear Chopin play, and getting from under that worn-out bruised nose like an indigestible hunk of Cheddar—getting a bolt of lightning, a revelation, strong enough to light up life *forever* from an entirely fresh viewpoint both inside and outside yourself.

"Hullo!"

"Hullo!"

We always met on the sloping windy street-corner by the police station. From this point the streets went off like dim-lit corridors in a large hotel, with dogs, milkbottles, shoes, etc. left outside the doors. Paving stones with mica sparkling in them led off to new liaisons.

"You're very Parisian, Guy."

"It's my coat. I got it in the flea market. It gives me a

long, French boy's waist. It's one of your long, thin days too, Sophie."

"On the contrary it's one of my short stumpy evenings. I'm at my shortest and stumpiest."

"You're waving about like a weeping willow."

"Stump, stump, stump. Here comes the district nurse."

"It's no good, Sophie, you're tall. So there."

"I'm *not*." My face fell.

"And heavy too, in fact. You've got heavy bones."

"Oh Guy, how could you. Call me a Roman Catholic, a racialist, anything. But tall and heavy!"

Oh the pleasure of re-entering childhood with Guy, and finding that my skin fitted me again, and that I was full of pert replies. I asked him:

"What were you telling Ruback about?"

"My ghost. I've only just realised it was a ghost, and even now I'm not sure …"

"Do tell me! I'm terrified already."

"You've got to take it seriously."

"Seriously? I'm a jelly of fear."

"Well, François had come over from the Cité Universitaire to spend the evening with me drinking Nescafé which we made on my kerosene stove …"

"Living it up in Paris in 1971."

"Honestly, Sophie, it's *grim* over there. Well, we must have drunk about twenty cups of the putrid stuff, and I walked back to the métro with him. And the métro stop is on the right bank at the end of one of those long stone bridges from the Île St Louis. So that meant I had to go back across the bridge alone, and find my way up to my bleak little room on the island. So far so good."

"What time was it?"

"It was eleven twenty-five, and it was a dry, sizzling

night, just like tonight ... in fact there was the same brownish light, and I was wearing this coat, and I had my finger through a hole in the pocket inside, just as I have now ..."

"How did you know the time so exactly?"

"Because in Paris I'm so on edge and nervous, I keep looking at my watch every few minutes, and making plans."

"Poor Guy!"

"François disappeared underground, and I turned back and started across the bridge, walking on the pavement close to the stone wall ... I saw someone coming towards me, walking in the road, just to my side of the crown of the road ... he was walking in a very leisurely way, and I took no notice of him really, until I was almost level with him, when I noticed that he was dressed in mid-nineteenth-century clothes. A frock-coat, a tall hat, and I particularly remember that the waistcoat was paler. I have the impression that he had gloves on, but I'm not sure. He was walking ... rather contemptuously, but it was an intellectual contempt, it wasn't real arrogance, not built-in. I thought it must be some eccentric from the left bank who'd dressed himself up and went about at night like that, to get attention. You know that people on the left bank will do *anything* to get attention ..."

"And *then*, Guy? What happened *then*?"

"Well, if you want to know I was absolutely terrified, really on the point of falling down, and my knees were knocking together. I prayed he wouldn't come towards me or look at me. And I bent my head and kept on by the wall, with my breath sort of bucketing in and out of my chest."

"But why was he so frightening?"

"Well, it was his face."

"His *face*! Oh God. What about his face?"

"It was the most unhealthy face I've ever seen. It wasn't

emaciated or anything. No. It was round, quite roundish, and it had a sickly white shine on it. My first thought was that he'd made it up with white cold cream to give it that ghastly look. It looked ... fishy. Phosphorescent. Or as though it had been buried in the ground for a few weeks, and had this gone-bad, luminous look."

"Guy!"

"I know. I told you you wouldn't believe me."

"But I *do*. That's what's so awful."

"Well, it's all true. I can see him in my mind right now, coming on looking ahead of him ... and me *praying* he wouldn't look at me. *And he did*."

I groaned. Guy was getting very agitated. He said:

"He *deliberately* turned towards me, and smiled sardonically ... not quite a smile, more of a grin. It was deliberately done in a knowing way to frighten the life out of me. He seemed to be saying: 'I know *you*. And what do you think you're doing out on the road at night, when the night and the road belong to me? You who are nothing and nobody, just a pawn, young and easily frightened.'"

"Oh hell."

"I looked away at once, because my greatest fear was that he would come towards me if I showed any sign of life. And I just kept on. I don't know how I got across that bridge, because on the other side of it I could hardly stand up. My knees were going out at all angles—like broken spokes in an umbrella."

"Did you look back?"

"*No!* I couldn't have looked back if you'd paid me a thousand pounds to do it. Suppose he'd *returned*?"

I looked over my shoulder for him. Guy said:

"I fled along the alleyways like a dying rat, with my heart beating about inside me, desperate to get indoors to the safety of my kerosene stove, my books, and the ticking of my Prisunic clock. I had to climb all the stairs of that lodging house, the Duc de Luynes, in the dark, except for the yellow strips under the doors. At the top, the stairs go into a spiral, and they're *cobbled*, so that you slip about. When I got in, I threw myself down on the hard bed and just lay there—I really thought my heart would get out, it was bounding about—it was like trying to keep a rabbit inside a box ..."

We both stopped, completely out of breath, goggling at one another in this draughty residential corridor. The hauntee and his confidante. High overhead a lamp was passing above the trees; made of red, green and white light, it moved over the house-tops, roaring to itself like a jinn. I could feel the vibration passing through my body and into the pavement.

"Guy, how did you know who it was on the bridge?"

"I had no idea at all. I just came to the conclusion that it was an eccentric, dressed-up. That is, until the end of July when I began to read Enid Starkie's life of Baudelaire. There's a photograph facing Page 433, and that's *him*. So is the painting by Courbet. The rest aren't."

"But are you *sure* you hadn't seen the photograph somewhere else?"

"Positive. I hadn't even read his poetry properly at that stage—just glanced at it. He didn't mean a thing to me, honestly. I can even remember what I was reading at the time—it was Boswell's *Life of Johnson*. So you see the sort of reasonable tack I was on."

"Not even in the right frame of mind for seeing things."

"Except that I was nervously keyed-up, couldn't sleep, no money, the usual things. And it's terribly lonely over there, you know. I was vulnerable."

"What did the ghost want?"

"He wanted to impress himself on me—young clay takes the print better. And the message was totally cynical. It wasn't a 'follow me' message. It was a quizzical, satirical: "you too?" It was a glance from the middle of the nineteenth century—and I was so glad to be alive *now*, and not then."

"You'll never know whether it was a ghost or not."

"If only I could trace his habits—but of course you'd need all the private details of a man's life. And this pale waistcoat of his is a nuisance, because there aren't any photographs of him in a pale waistcoat."

"You could check up on the bridges. Has that bridge always been there?"

"Don't know. God, I feel cold."

"That's because you walk with your shoulders hunched up to keep the ghosts off. Try putting them back."

"I've had them back."

Guy shook out his lion's mane in disgust. Coffee was what he wanted; everyone knows that after making love or telling ghost stories a hot drink is *essential*. He chattered his teeth at me like a performer who's done his turn and needs a reward, so I took him into the Coffee Cup. I was impressed by his story, and we found we needed to eat some solid buns with white glass on them, baked only that morning, to munch our way back to normal.

"These buns are excellent!"

"They're the best buns in Europe!"

"What buns!"

"Sustaining, nourishing, pure buns!"

"We don't want to be late."

"God no. We know what that means."

Certainly we knew what that meant. The "late stragglers" would have to pay for it. They would be given a quiet but thorough psychological tarring and feathering by indirect means. There would be dark hints about those who expected to be given the keys of Heaven and, in return, couldn't perform the simplest task that was asked of them (i.e. get to a lecture on time). These would be sprinkled over the solid, luminous discourse like black pepper, so look out!

When we stepped out on the way to our party again, Guy suddenly drew back and hid himself in a doorway. What was it? More ghosts? It was so like Rudolf Horner ducking down to hide from his ex-wife in Princess Melika's front garden that you wanted to say to Nature: "Not again! We've just had all that in the father." It was established, then, that hide-and-seek was in the family.

"Is that my father's car?" This persecuted hiss-whine came out of his hair, while he tried at the same time to hide in it. "The parked one, with the windows rolled up. Over *there*."

He was like a kettle on the boil in the African bush. So I hissed back like another kettle:

"*No!* Hiss, hiss. It is *not*. Hiss, hiss, hiss."

He cowered there for a minute, and then came out, more hunched than ever.

"He's been following me, you know. Ever since mother told him I'd gone mystical. I haven't got a bit of privacy; between the two of them, they're shaking all the life out of me. Why don't they leave me alone? I just want to be myself."

"They want you to improve life for them. And you're not doing it. They want you to *do* something. And you just want to *be*. It's the most selfish thing they've ever heard of!"

"If only Father weren't quite so—the silly thing is that in a way I admire him. But I can't bear to be with him. He embarrasses me all the time."

"Philip says the same." I managed to say the name in a commonplace tone, but Guy at once knew something was wrong. If he hadn't heard already.

"Oh—Philip. He's so successful, but so hard. I can't talk to him any more. He's going in the opposite direction, turning himself into a perfect little Englishman. Whereas I'm going *back* … to being a continental—and a dropout, too, in their language. Philip's going West and I'm going East. If only Father would stop driving us!"

"Guy, do tell me, I've never dared to ask. What was Philip's mother like? I never knew her."

"Father was *terrified* of her. He's always quoted as having made one famous remark to her: 'Don't intimidate me, Muriel, so that I do *pipi* in my trousers.' You see the kind of father I've got!"

"Oh Guy. It's so funny—and touching."

"It is not touching. It's bloody wet. In all senses."

"Were they married long?"

"No. A matter of days I'm told. Just long enough to make Philip legitimate."

"But she must have had some feeling for him. After all, she left him the yellow sofa."

There was a crazy burst of laughter from Guy, quite coarse and out of character.

"The one Pussy's got? Of course she left him the yellow sofa. It was *revenge*."

"Revenge for what?"

"Oh the usual things. Making love to her and marrying her … and everyone else within reach. Father eats other people's cake for them, you know. He'd like to eat *mine*, right now." Guy flashed out more suspicious glances at the traffic, all very bitter and withering.

"I still don't see how leaving him a sofa …"

"It depends what *happened* on the sofa," said Guy luridly, "or rather, what *didn't* happen. You see, there's one thing I will say for my father and that is he has excellent taste in furniture. It's only when sex comes into it that he loses his head. He's just a womaniser. He's just a damn silly kisser of women. Did you notice what a big lump of a sofa it was? And bright yellow?"

"Dirty yellow."

"Well, it's been sitting in Pussy's north room, you know. That takes the pollen off you."

"And so?"

"And so it's got unhappy memories for Father. That's why it's in Pussy's north room. Everything ends up in Pussy's north room."

"It isn't. It's out in the open. And Rudi wants it; he's going to take it away from her."

Guy was delighted. He shook his head over this piece of news with disgusted gratification, as he always did when something confirmed him in his opinion of his father. He waited patiently for me to run him down so that he could then fly to his protection; he wanted to be glum and to ponder his wretched heredity. In the end he had to start the running-down on his own, hoping I would join in.

"So he's taking it away from Pussy! A useless piece of furniture he doesn't even want. And which he *hates*. He's so damn greedy and grasping it makes me sick. He's got a house full of furniture in the country, a house full of furniture in Hampstead, and a shop full of furniture in Mount Street."

"And I'm told he's going to leave you the lot!"

Guy stood absolutely still on the pavement in order to make a statement. It was another piece of broadcasting; oh dear.

"*I* shan't outlive Father. He'll bury us all. He's got all the sex, all the instinct, all the animal soul. He'll even bury *Philip*. And that's saying something."

At the sound of the beloved name once more that evening at a moment when I hadn't expected it, I tottered as though pushed over by an amorous whirlwind. Guy stood there with his personal problems dragging him down, putting a slope on his shoulders, oozing out of his ears; a thoroughly wrecked human being, a worrier and seer of ghosts. We were both ripe for eternity at thirty-one and twenty-two.

Dark forms were passing us, and friendly greetings were getting in through our private fog. We were *there* ... we had only to go up the steps, and listen, and gradually all these burdens would vanish. Our guilt and fear and isolation would leave us. And endless horizons would be opened for us. We would be taught how to live and how to die. We would be *in control* of circumstances.

"Come on!" said Guy joyfully.

We went up the steps, hunting in our pockets for twenty pence in silver each. I rang the low press-button doorbell; it wasn't any bigger than a pearl button. We could hear the zing of it going along on the other side of the dimpled glass, and then feet hurrying to let us in. Life!

6

Philip would ring me up as though nothing had happened. At first this was incomprehensible to me; my tongue stuck in my mouth, I had nothing to say. Then I returned to my old way of chattering. I realised that something curious had come about. He had become emotionally dependent on me, without even knowing it. What he must have said to himself logically was that there was no need to put an end to a happy relationship. He needed and took my thoughts and comments for three-quarters of an hour on the phone every day in order to balance his mind. Or rather, he could give me his mind and rest it, knowing that I wouldn't attack or needle him, or be contradictory for the sake of it. I knew that I had discovered a deep emotional weakness in him, and that I must look after him, because he did not understand himself. I suddenly realised that he could crash; and that he hadn't even an ounce of Guy's psychological strength. I loved him twice as much, three times as much.

But it held me back.

The trouble was those three barren sentences spoken in the hotel room had taken away my dignity and self-respect. As a proposal of non-marriage, half-baked and half-hearted, it was the most beastly, drab little speech ever made to me. It ran so against our actions and feelings together that my brain simply boiled when I heard it. The butterfly wings I had been wearing to attract him, the cosmetics, the moods, the mirrors I had looked into, the sophistication to handle life in order to make it amusing, these wings that only needed to be dipped in a cocktail to clean them and keep them magical and powdered were of no value at all to Philip. A good strong grey mackintosh with ventilation holes in the armpits and worn preferably with a matching hat as terrible as a pudding-bowl, were what his soul wanted. Because only a woman with a very great deal of money could afford to dress like that.

Philip adored smartness; and it was always smart to wear a grey mackintosh and to be very rich at the same time. He would simply go on looking until he found the two together. And all my up-to-the-minute jokes about the current fashions were useless. My: "Are we going to a party? Oh good, I'll just run down to an old drag-shop in the Tottenham Court Road and ask them if they have any old worn-out mustard-coloured dressing-gowns, preferably with torn linings," this was so much empty headed chirruping. He didn't know how it came about. Above all, he didn't know why he wanted it so much; enough to phone up every day for it. I made a special kind of energy, a style of life, he lacked and envied. He tore my wings, and tore my personality, on the basis that my offer was not good enough. But—behind the fact that I simply hadn't any money—was another much more interesting fact. Philip was fighting a personality war with me.

In rudimentary terms it's the war of the half-developed against the more fully-developed human being. The war of dogs against people. The dogs want to level down those who have more style, more energy, more reality. A television set is an object made by dogs for dogs, on which dogs appear and wag their tails. If a real person turns up on the screen there's pandemonium and you can hear the barking half way across the world. Most people want to return to the dog from which they came because it's so much easier to go back.

Philip, who was so brilliantly clever mentally, so instinctive physically, did not seem to have a spiritual element in his composition. It did not exist in the modern world in which he moved, and he himself couldn't supply it. And so when he was cornered on that level by my thoughts, he behaved like a dog to me. He destroyed me to protect himself. If only he had used a different set of words, and a little more understanding! But he broadcast an honest message in the language of the dogs' television set. And I fell from a great height: and instantly grew up.

From that day he wooed me harder than ever. He left me notes which said: "Thank you for being so sweet." He seemed to be trying to give me, in love and appreciation, all that he had held back in spoken words. But I wanted the dignity he had taken away from me. And that he couldn't give me. He had shown me into his head, and there was my name on the short list for execution at such-and-such a date.

The main difficulty in my life now was to stop loving someone I loved. It was like not loving my mother. People don't say: "Are you still seeing your mother?"

We still went to parties together. But now I began, for the first time, to observe him. To start with I had a very good look at him. He had a fine cold milk skin, from which the early lines, only pencilled in by hard work, seemed to be disappearing. His eyes were dark brown, marvellous, interested, highly erotic, between milky eyelids with dense lashes and below thick eyebrows with a curl to them which I had never noticed before. His eyes looked out with absolute self-confidence. His dark hair had always been prolific, like Guy's, and now he wore it very slightly longer than he should have done. The body inside his shirt was becoming *almost* bulky. He was so attractive to women that you could see a chain reaction of interested glances go across a room from the moment he entered it. He knew this, took it for granted, and sunned himself in his own radiant heat. It was only just lately that he had begun to talk with his body half into a group and half out of it. And to stroke down the hair on the back of his head with his arm sticking out selfishly as though he was still at home leaning on a chimney breast. As a bachelor who is completely free, he gave himself the right to look over your shoulder while he talked to you, having decided that you would put up with it. He seemed to be at the height of his sensual development.

With a shock I realised that the young Hermes now knew his sexual power and *had begun to be smart in his person*. No wonder he had privately decided he would no longer need me. He had been learning from me: how to stand, how to ignore, how to be weary, how to attract. Without bothering to learn how to dress he had become, quite simply, a danger to women. And I had been the agent in this transformation; night after night my body, slight and anxious to please, had taught this large clever body how to play.

I was much envied. Because his careful habits didn't change. He still waited for me without complaining. He was loyal to me; he put himself out to please me, to keep me. I turned the light out in my brain ... and after a while, we went to bed again. I loathed myself.

Then I woke up one day and found that I had begun to dislike him. It was like a birthday present! I got up and cooked an enormous breakfast. While I ate the bacon and eggs, I opened the kitchen window—how loudly the birds were singing!

Like lightning, I realised what was happening to Philip. His body was beginning to take over. He had been able to keep his father out of his mind, but he could not keep him out of his body. It was worse than being haunted. In spite of all his care, his rejection of me, his ambition, and his integrity, his father was reappearing, incarnate *in his flesh.* And he could do nothing about it.

I'd reached a point when I had to free myself. I seemed to be sinking more deeply every day into layers and layers of sugar icing; Philip's telephone calls, gifts, flowers, letters, meetings. I thought of Mr Ruback, who had taught me how to *see* Philip as a whole; but he was distant. I didn't feel I could approach him. And his answer must surely be that there was enough in his lectures to show me the way. And so there was. But I was sinking too fast to be able to rescue myself. Then I thought of Pussy and phoned her.

"You must go straight to Willie Broughton!"

"Who, Pussy?"

"Willie Broughton. A marvellous clairvoyant. He knows it all. Go tomorrow. Just a minute, I'll look up his number ... B, B, B, B, ... B ... Here we are: Broughton 733105 Brighton."

"Brighton? That's half a day."

"Do you want a life or don't you?"

"I do."

"Well, *hurry up* then. You're dithering."

"I suppose I'm afraid he'll tell me something unpleasant."

"He will *know* what to tell you. He's wise and kind. You need something to get you out of that rut. I don't know how you could have let yourself sink so low. And I've been hearing such great things about your Mr Ruback!"

"They're all true, Pussy. But for the lectures Philip would have completely destroyed me."

A "phooey" noise down the phone. Melika said:

"Philip? He's still a little child. You know that ... we talked about it together. Have you forgotten?"

"Oh no. I can remember every word."

"Remember I told you: 'he's yours if you want him'? It's still true."

"Oh no, it isn't. I've been rejected; and he still won't leave me alone."

"It's his head, his stupid ambitious intelligence. That's always been Philip's trouble. He doesn't trust his heart. But he'll never let you go, believe me. If he sees signs of you getting away, there will be a *frightful* to-do ... he'll be round with a proposal before dark."

"But I don't want that now!"

"Ah!" Pussy made some typical noises. "Aha! Now we're getting to the truth. Tell me something: weren't you really rather *relieved* ... when he said something nasty to you? Because he did, didn't he? He's the type who would."

"Well, in a funny way, slightly. Because it meant that I could get on with something that interested me. I could follow up my work in archeology. And I've always wanted to learn Russian, your language, Pussy."

Melika said dramatically:

"In other words you had already passed him on the road."

"But I'm not using the time. I'm languishing. I'm painting my bathroom, of all things!"

"Of course you are." Nothing could surprise Pussy today. Being right into one end of the telephone receiver and getting confirmation of you rightness straight away from the other end is as good as the Elixir of Life or some other Olympic Old Lady's drink on a winter day. "You're dithering about painting bathrooms, because Philip is a psyche-stealer."

Oh God, more wisdom.

"Hmm."

"Don't you feel dead tired, drained, after you've been with him?"

"Well, yes, actually. But …"

"You feel as though you've been stopping up a hole in the universe, dancing about like a little puppet, saying 'pretty polly'?"

"Yes, but …"

"Whatever you give to Philip it will never be enough. If you gave him Paris, he would ask for Moscow, like Napoleon."

This was so true that I didn't even bother to agree. I grumbled:

"He's begun to talk on the telephone as well."

"Just like a woman!" croaked Pussy, who had developed the telephone conversation as a substitute for life in Paris and Moscow. "Just like his father!" She suddenly became powerful again. "Listen to me. You've got to get the smell of this man out of your nostrils. Brighton first; and then Normandy—you'll love it, there are five children with black eyes."

New life seemed to be pouring down the telephone.

"May I …?"

"May you! May you! Stop playing the little girl, it's too sickly. You know you're as hard as a man."

"Oh!" That brought me up short. So that was what was the matter. I wasn't a proper woman. That is what life with my mother had done for me. My masculine childhood was against me. "I see."

"That's why I'm not really worried about you. It's Philip I'm worried about … it's this awful virility. Promise me: you'll be very, very gentle with him?"

I didn't know whether I was on my head or my heels; I reeled. While I was looking for the right answer, the telephone said firmly:

"Never mind. I know you will." There was a curious clink, rather like a knife on a china plate. I asked suspiciously:

"Pussy, what are you doing?"

"Just cutting myself a piece of cake." (Muffled cake-eating growls) "Now off to Brighton with you." No wonder she was indestructible; if someone bored her on the telephone, she simply ate cake. I said wearily:

"Was there ever a bit of your life that went right, Pussy?"

"Yes, the bit I had with Ziz."

"I think I've already had that bit with Philip."

* * *

I phoned Willie Broughton. There was so much fear, anticipation, and fervency in my voice that it throbbed like a wood pigeon; no one could have sounded more clairvoyant. I ought to have consulted myself.

An Irish voice said thoughtfully over the phone:

"You've got a very beautiful speaking voice. No, don't tell me your name. I don't want to know who you are. I don't see many people these days. But I feel I'd like to see you."

And so it was arranged in two or three sentences. The following Saturday I went down on the Brighton Belle. Fifty-six minutes from Victoria, and I passed them sitting transfixed in the hot carriage. Wasn't I doing something rather dangerous? What right had I to ask for direct help? Especially when a whole way of life, *the* way, had been given to me by Mr Ruback. After all I wasn't having a nervous breakdown.

Or was I? Isn't wasting time, living on savings, painting

bathrooms, a form of nervous breakdown? Isn't buying new lampshades a form of slow death? And I remembered that even while doing that last week, I said to myself: "How can I go out and buy lampshades when my heart is breaking?"

But suppose the Unknown paid me back? Death by drowning. Or a long, painful illness. Or a plane crash, trying to fly to somewhere hopeless like Perpignan to please Philip. Or quicksand.

At the thought of the quicksand, I could feel brown mud stuffing itself into my nostrils. I got up quickly and tried to open the little window with two metal latches which ventilated the carriage; it took me straight back to the hotel bedroom. After another struggle of the same sort—but this time sideways instead of up and down and using an entirely new set of muscles—I pressed it open six inches and blew out the quicksand.

Then I went over the papers I'd brought with me. Rather as though I was setting out to see a strange doctor, I'd assembled some articles which had a part in my case history: a letter from Philip, a letter from the Languages School asking me to return, a short sermon on Christianity versus drug-taking by my mother, my lecture notes on mysticism, a photograph of a château in Normandy given to me by Princess Melika.

I found I was anxious about the house itself. I imagined a ghostly place with tables quietly rapping on themselves in distant rooms, owls hooting, black cats, skulls, and above all, necromancer's cobwebs.

These childish imaginings came off in transfers in my head, but I knew that I would go through with it. There was no doubt at all in my mind. The only single thing I could think of to safeguard myself against a flow of unpleasant prophecy was to ask him to limit himself to the next two years. I had an idea, though, after listening to Mr Ruback, that a clairvoyant's time sense was not reliable and his predictions haphazard.

I don't know how many people have gone down on the Brighton Belle to see Willie Broughton, but I imagined that they were all people who knew their minds better than I did. I was ashamed, for example, that my mind was so susceptible to fresh experience, to novelty. Out of courtesy to my mother it contained also a great deal of her superstitious fearfulness, and a guilt factory that controlled my movements. When something happened to me and I stopped still to assess it—I realised the experience had come up against a piece of her mind inside me, had been weighed for importance, graded for good or evil, and sorted away before I could even get hold of it. I had only just begun to break down this secondhand market in my mind, as a result of Mr Ruback's teaching. No wonder my mother feared him. He would separate us ... and I would cross over from my mother's sofa to Pussy's sofa, because Pussy lived so that she and her friends could fulfil their potential, their chase and search for the blue poppy, and my mother lived for herself and myself. And that wasn't enough for me.

Before I got out of the train I remembered all the stories people had told me—in husky whispers in the middle of parties, or over dimly-lighted restaurant tables—about predictions made to them. And not one of them had ever said to me: "And not a word of it came true." A woman who was told she would inherit a library, and thirty years later was left a political library in Rome. A man who was told he would have a stupendous success in Hollywood as a film designer, and had done so. A woman who was told she would have a son much later in life, and go to live far away from her own country: all this occurred.

I suddenly pulled myself together. The contents of my mind appalled me. I was behaving, mentally, as though I was still at one of those parties. What a rubbishy background against which to test what Broughton would say to me. If I couldn't make the landscape inside my head firm and serious, how could I expect to launch a proper life from there? And how could I expect a stranger, a clairvoyant, to give me a serious reading, when I didn't take myself seriously? No wonder I was so badly equipped to make decisions. It was obvious to me at once that I must broaden my education, discipline myself, and return to exact standards.

Jolt! Brighton.

I emerged from the carriage in a hard, realistic frame of mind, as though getting over a hangover; everything had an edge. There were a great many seaside taxis with seats inside them as plump as bath buns. I was forcibly fed white fresh air as I got the back door of one of them open. Once inside, it was like being bundled along very quietly on air cushions, and hot, with a head and neck of grimy, elderly seaman's skin to look at. The effect was soporific, like the rocking of a cradle, and was so irresistible I could almost have dozed off; at this all-important moment in my life!

Yes, he knew Mr Broughton. Out at Hove, wasn't it? I was firmly on the psychic conveyor-belt now. We passed through very slow traffic; the cars travelled at the same pace as cows and made equivalent noises. No one hurried.

We arrived. There was a detached suburban house set down below the level of the road and looking rather damp. It had all the desperate suburban attachments: a wrought-iron gate which squealed "eeeee" and tiled steps going down quite steeply to a minute forecourt of that crazy paving which I thought had gone out of existence years ago.

Over the front door hung a fancy lantern with yellow panes. I rang the bell, which turned out to be a loud tradesman's brrrr! No one answered. I had time to look down at some wet plants, which were hanging flabby leaves with crimson veins on the undersides that made them look like cold meat, in the brown frowsty beds around the house. I was in the act of ringing the bell again when the door opened silently.

Now that was the very first impression from the inside of the house: silence. A large soft elderly man stood there. He was formal, and showed me, like a very quiet dentist, into a large sitting-room deep inside. Then he closed the door and left me alone. I assessed the chairs; one was obviously *his*—that blue high-backed one which enclosed you like a sedan-chair, on the left of the fireplace—and this low, horsehair and leather one on the right was surely for visitors. I sat on it, and looked with curiosity at the middle-class objects, the china, the silver and brass, a great deal of it, all polished and in good condition. A little clock was ticking rapidly. There was a gleaming yellow brass fire-surround with a pattern of triangles punched in the metal. I had an impression of ornamental brown Victorian wallpaper, possibly with a flock finish. Certainly the room was quite full up. A great many shiny expensive objects had been acquired by its owner, who wasn't at all badly off. It was not unlike one of those misnamed antique shops in the heart of the country, where a room has been got together to show off the wares but has not actually been lived in.

Again the door opened silently. Mr Broughton joined me. He sat down in the blue chair and my session with the supernatural began.

"Now I want you to give me something of yours which you carry on you all the time, and which you've had for at least a year."

"My watch?"

"Yes, your watch will do very well."

I unclipped it and handed it to him over the low fireside table. A very soft hand took it from me.

He held it up a little, against his chest, and there was absolute silence between us. Then he began to speak lightly.

"There's a man here. He's a very good man. But you must be very careful with him. He did want to marry you, and you did want to marry him, but ..." (he made a dismissive gesture) "... he can't keep his mind on it."

"Oh. I see." I didn't want to confirm, or, alternatively, block what he had to say. But in spite of my caution, in a few minutes I was to be talking naturally to him, because he seemed to be in possession of all the facts of my life.

Mr Broughton said:

"One day he wants you, and next day he's off away somewhere else in his thoughts, and you don't exist. When he *does* love you, I think he loves you more than you love him." I shook my head. "He really loves you. But—he can't keep it up. And this is *built into him*. He can't help it. And I don't think he's going to change. Now now."

I listened, dumb, to the Irish voice.

"Now this has been a very *good* thing, on the whole. It's been a very happy relationship." (I nodded) "And I think that when you come to add up the gains and losses, you'll find after all—gain." He thought for a minute and said in an interested voice: "You know, I've only come upon his kind of personality very rarely, and it's always been ... in seamen ... or people who have been at sea for a long time and have got out of touch ..."

It was at that point I remembered I had a letter of Philip's with me. It might be that from this Willie Broughton could explain the strong velvet chain between us, which we couldn't break. I didn't care to interrupt him, but he was already (so quick) looking at me and waiting for me to speak.

"I've got a letter of his. If that's any use?"

"Oh do give it to me," he said warmly. His eyes with their shiny walls of blue looked at me.

I went into my fleshy, leather shoulder-bag with its purple silk lining and purple zip-fasteners sealing up the secret pockets. In there were all the documents I'd brought with me. But however much I zipped and unzipped those pockets, I could not find the precious letter from Philip. I stared into the bag, defeated. My entire future was staked on that letter which was concealing itself from my fingers. How could it not be there, when I *knew* it was there?

Willie Broughton said with absolute conviction:

"It was not meant to be."

"But it's here somewhere."

"Never mind. We'll go on without it."

"It's so crazy. Because I had it in my hand."

He waited for me to calm down because I was obviously such a tyro in dealing with the invisible world. The letter was being concealed from me; the letter was not to be my fate. And I persisted in behaving as though visible, tangible objects could not vanish, or have a life of their own. He let me look for it, though, knowing I wouldn't find it. At last he said patiently.

"It was not to be, my dear young lady. There is no such thing as chance. Let me go on with what there is in here." He again concentrated on my watch. "You've only just emerged from the smog yourself, and have come out into life. And now you're out you're going to *stay* out. Are you good at languages? Because you should be. That's where your future lies."

"Well, not bad."

"But you're not doing enough of it!" he said with great force, suddenly becoming my father. "I see a great future going out to other people in other tongues. Great luxury and wealth. Another man, a man from the past, is going to be important to you again. A connection with another country, and that will be a great and wonderful thing." He smiled almost to himself.

"Oh." There was to be something for me then, after all. I could have wept with relief. I had begun to think that only Philip was entitled to a future.

"You should have done *much more* at your age, with all you've got in here." He meant the energy buried inside the wristwatch. "He's been holding you back, you know." He meant Philip: and suddenly, as though reaching the centre of the relationship, and observing all the motives which met together there, he said emphatically: "He wants to have you. And break you down. And make you into just an ordinary woman. And what's that? Nothing."

Not a word of this surprised me; it was as though my own subconscious had found a voice, and now knew what it was up to.

"No, my dear young lady. This is not right for you." He paused. "I think you know it anyway. Because I see a 'mental weeping.' Behind every action you do—even if it's only buying a loaf of bread—it takes you all your strength to do it because you are crying inside. Now, you must stop all that. Because you've got so much love and affection coming to you. But you must get out of your rut. You're too much of an idealist."

Again, against my caution, I burst out:

"Oh I should have given him up long ago."

"No," said Willie Broughton deeply, "because he *was* your life, and you *were* his life. But now I'm telling you to leave him, because he won't leave you. He *wants* you. I don't care how you do it, but do it gently." He looked at me. "You're a bit psychic yourself, you know. I see colours over your head. You've been on this planet before. You won't have a nervous breakdown now, because great strength is indicated here." Without warning he returned to the subject of Philip, who seemed to interest him very much: "If I were to go into a room full of strangers, *he* is the one I would want to talk to. He's got fantastic concentration. He would make a very good friend to a man, but he will never be any good to any woman."

I said faintly:

"I get—a loss of personality—after I've been with him."

"You would do," he said energetically, "because he hasn't the slightest idea what makes you tick. God was certainly looking after you when he didn't let you make a baby by that man. But he wants to have one by you."

I was shaken by this antiquated way of putting it, because Philip had been quite happy for me to have a baby, whether or not it would decide things between us. It might have forced us into a temporary unification, just as it must have done in his mother's case. Was that the work of the yellow sofa?

"Now, you," Willie Broughton was speaking again, "will always be misunderstood in your work and your personality. Because you put up such a terrific show. Pay no attention to this; just go on with your work. Because the people who matter will get through to you; they will come to you. Because you're a mental giver. You have the gift of understanding."

He stopped again and seemed to look inward.

"I see a flag of the stars and stripes fluttering in the breeze. I see colour and cameras, and black faces. I see people digging in the sand among old ruins of fallen masonry ... you're there ... I can see you walking about ... you like it there. You're going to meet a whole new set of people. People of wealth and influence will change your life. Everything is changing. All very worthwhile. Anything you do from now on will be successful; and any friendships you make will be *lasting* ... But it will come to you in another language."

I groaned; it all seemed light-years away.

"Don't lose heart," he said sympathetically. "You can't go on before you're ready. You couldn't have got on any faster before because you were helping other people."

I had a picture of my mother, shipwrecked over the ironing board and calling out: "Stop! Stop! Oh my stomach muscles!"

He bent, as though completely fagged out, and placed my watch on the table.

"That's all I see."

He lay back in his blue chair, resting. He must have been over seventy, and I realised that it had been a strain on him. I wanted to restore him and to apologise.

"I'm so sorry. I've taken all your strength away."

"Oh no you haven't. It's just that I have circulation trouble."

"But it must be a great strain ..."

"Good heavens, no. When I was a young man I couldn't see enough people. Directly one had left the room, I was *on my toes* waiting for the next to come in. As it is, I'm all right now down to there," he chopped at his waistline with his hand, "but the rest isn't getting the blood to it."

"Are you on your own here?"

There wasn't a sound, but for running tick-tick-tick of the little clock.

"Oh no. I'm surrounded by helpers," he said happily. "I've had a lovely life."

He was completely contented! A man of his intelligence sitting in a room papered with brown Victorian flock, crammed with brass and silver ornaments with so little taste that you could begin a whole new idea of taste from the tastelessness, all alone in a damp suburban house outside Brighton, he was happy! I loved him, and couldn't help smiling over and over again at him. Not only was he happy, he was convinced that he had had "a lovely life." And he was right; because I had previously been looking at his possessions, his house, his life, his silence, through Philip's critical eyes. And now, when I looked again, I saw them differently. I saw a man of great majesty, spiritually a giant, who was living *at ease* still inside the class into which he had been born, and having no necessity whatsoever to climb out of it and interest himself in the next layer of Persian pottery, T'ang horses, and Georgian candelabra, bowls of flowers on polished tables and nicely dressed people discussing one another or the Royal Family. He had no necessity because all classes were equal and came *to him*; it not only enabled him to be true to himself, but confirmed his personality—if he hadn't reached the stage where personality ceases to exist or matter. So he didn't trouble himself about superficial questions but mixed an atmosphere in which he could develop himself. And the result sat facing me, calm, triumphant, radiating wisdom and goodness. I no longer heard—with my pricked up metropolitan ears—the silence as something threatening, as an admission of an empty, defeated life, but as the proper element *for life*, in which people and things could be themselves.

He began to tell me about his twin brother who had died, I think, at the age of eight, but continued to advise him from "the other world." Then he looked at me carefully and said, "I'm going to tell you something about myself that I've never told anyone." And he told me about his early life and marriage. After a moment I saw that he was showing me, by analogy, a way of living through my present emotional difficulties, and giving me a lesson in how to protect myself from other human beings who became too predatory. He had done so, and survived.

It occurred to me that this interview had contained very little actual fortune-telling, but had isolated and clarified my great problem so that I was already *ahead*, looking back on it as a whole unit, with disinterested interest. He had managed to get the stake out of my heart without any pain.

It is very hard to leave the presence of a man who has done you some great psychological benefit, because you begin to feel so well physically. You put yourself together in his light. And want to stay on and on, growing and learning. But you also know when you've been given enough. And not wanting to be greedy, I was about to get up to go.

"Shall I phone for a taxi for you?" asked Willie Broughton.

"Yes please."

I was back on the conveyor-belt with all the other visitors. Then there was the question of payment. Melika had said five guineas, but she wasn't sure.

I took out my cheque-book and, bending over it, I thought it would be polite to hide a financial question under my hair. I asked timidly:

"Is it—five guineas?"

It was. Scribble scribble. The same fee as that of my mother's Harley Street doctors, who did her so little good, but allowed her to describe her symptoms and habits without calling out: "Stop!" The same price as the trichologist who banged her head about like an old broom, and then poured on some icy cold stuff. Each one of us had a way of getting what we needed. I had been dipped, baked, in the supernatural for half an hour and was feeling much better for it. Evidently I was not so different from my mother after all.

I replaced my watch and Willie Broughton came to the door with me, saying paternally:

"Now with all the strength I've just given you, you can do all the things you really want to do. And *must* do. So please get on with it. Because you're wasting yourself."

He gently pressed both my hands in his with a sort of loving politeness as we stood on the front porch under the yellow-paned lantern. I had never seen a face so lit up by two sparkling eyes with the cut-brightness of mountain water. I heard the taxi pull up, and, as I looked towards it, I felt a kiss dashed on my cheek. This elderly man wished me well, and had given me a life, fresh hope, and my self-respect back again, and sealed it as my own father might have done.

"Good luck!" he said, as actors do to one another before going off to start a new part.

He was gone into his door, and I was up the stairs with his "good luck" in my head, to join all the other living voices that once called "good luck" to me along school corridors before an examination as I held my lucky grey fountain pen, or before a new job, or a long railway journey, or the first evening out with a man.

I took the taxi to the front at Brighton, and then got out and paid it off. I wanted ... to damp down my new strength, in case it burnt a hole in my side. I took a short meandering walk over the gravel-stone beach. I went down to the lip of the sea and stared at it; it banged the ground at my feet, luminous and heavy. I watched the soft drag-boil of grey water. It had left cold pools about, the colour of soap froth, potatoes, lice. I felt safe inside and very happy. Far out the light went on and off.

There were silver onions and other silver lids on Brighton pier; in the green rooms underneath gallons of dark fishy water chopped about. If you stood still for long here, the sea would get inside you and clean you out like a whistle. It begins with the wind going past your ears in that continuous alleluia that cherubim are supposed to sing ... and then the coarse electric staring of the sea keeps you wide awake ...

Yes, make a bachelor life for yourself again. Get away from all this nauseating emotion. Stop furnishing your flat with the equivalent of the yellow sofa to please Philip. Take up your studies, go back to the Languages School and begin to widen your circle. You are just beginning to know a few people; when you answer letters, think more carefully and be responsible, prepare reasons and try to be sure they are based on your inner feelings. Bring the mystical teaching naturally into your daily life. When you have built yourself into a certain sort of person, you attract to you others of similar type. And then, who knows? "A whole new set of people." "Another man."

The idea that someone might take a liking to me, someone rather nice, and with no worldly reason in mind, this simple, childish idea filled me with amazement and joy.

Turning away refreshed, I remembered Philip's missing letter. In the cold sea-wind, I opened the shoulder-bag and went through it, bewildered. Then I laughed out loud. Have you forgotten? It was so important, that letter of Philip's, that you put it separately in a skin pocket outside, where you could get to it in a second if necessary without having to rummage through the interior.

So I had concealed the letter from myself.

7

"There were five bloods coming down the road, all singing at the tops of their voices: 'I'm going to dig a hole and pee in it!'" said Rudi.

"Does this happen every night in Mayfair?" asked my mother, deeply interested.

"Yes, every damn night if you're not careful. And they come and pee on *my* doorstep. So I got Hitchin to stand behind the door with a bucket of water, and I went up to the first floor with another bucket of water. And after we had waited for them for *hours*, they went and peed in the drain, damn it!"

Luckily Rudi was in the front seat of the car and my mother and I were in the back, so I was able to stop these two trouble-makers going too far.

Hitchin was driving. He wore a green uniform and sometimes took part in the conversation. He was only really dangerous—from the talking point of view—when Rudi lent you the car and you were alone with him. Then he grinned with violent joy and talked non-stop, just like Rudi; and you got out of the car reeling about stone blind drunk with it.

Today he was intimidated by the three of us, and kept quiet. Besides we were going along country lanes with high grassy banks, and you had to keep the nose of this big brute of a car just so. Inside the car it was like a little sitting-room. We were all in high spirits; this is how all weekends begin. They end with insomnia, madness, and a little black liver spot that travels about near the end of your nose.

"You should have emptied a bag of flour over them!" said my mother. "And then the police could have picked them out."

"We thought of that," said Rudi, who had always thought of everything, "but it's not so easy to get the flour over them."

"Suppose they got it in their eyes? Or suppose one of them had asthma?" I asked.

"Serve them right," said Rudi. "I've got a lot of very valuable furniture there. I can't have people peeing all over the steps."

"The way young people express themselves nowadays!" My mother laughed happily. "It's simply frightful."

"It's simply *awful*," said Rudi. "Do you know that during the whole time Guy was in Paris I only had one card from him? And do you know what that one card said?"

"No. What?"

"'*We're all pissed over here.*'" He looked at us with burning dramatic eyes, fulfilled in his suffering as a father.

"Oh, it's just a young boy's way of expressing himself," said my mother, giving me an entirely different message by contracting her eyelid and the corner of her mouth in my direction.

"He is not a young boy. He is twenty-two years old. He is *a man*. And what is this man doing? He is playing at being a Red Indian."

"It's a sickness of the soul," said my mother with more compression around the mouth for me, and looking very contented to think that she hadn't got it.

"Rudi, he is *not* playing at being a Red Indian," I said, "he's just trying to find a meaning in life before being sucked under—like you, Rudi."

Rudi took his pause over the top of the leather seat like a ventriloquist waiting for his doll to speak. He said gravely:

"You are very much mistaken if you think I am 'sucked under,' my dear. I assure you that is the last thing that will ever happen to me. But Guy is a different matter. I am very gloomy about that boy. He has no sense of direction in his life."

"But that's exactly what he has got!"

"No. None at all. What is going to happen to him when he has to run my business? What does it mean to him if this is a Biedermeier sofa and that is a Louis Quinze armchair? All he wants is to have Red Indians all over the place, peeing on the steps ... he would most probably go out and pee with them."

Even my mother glanced at Hitchin this time. Rudi at once began to laugh, pleased to think he'd gone too far.

"Don't worry. He is used to it. Aren't you, Hitchin?"

"Yes, sir." Hitchin drove with exquisite tact, his lids dropped half over his eyes as if he was in another room reading a newspaper, as motionless as a lizard. Except when he was talking, of course, when his jaws were happily on the move all the time. Rudi was not in control of him, any more than he was in control of his housekeeper, Mrs Wynne. Rudi wanted to explain things more fully to my mother. He said:

"You see the trouble with Guy is that everything has been too easy for him. He has not the slightest idea of what life is all about."

The self-satisfied expression on his face and on my mother's face very nearly made me ill. I thought of Guy crawling back to the companionship of a Prisunic clock on the Île St Louis and myself groping my way around a dark hotel bedroom: both of us the tortured children of these smug marionettes.

"Well, what is it, Sophie? You sit there looking so disapproving."

Rudi was excitable and spoiling for a fight. He had nothing else to do at the moment, and wanted to find common ground with my mother. This was done by showing her his values, sound and permanent objects, and then admiring them in front of her. But you need someone to disagree with you and ruffle you, because only then are you suddenly and wholeheartedly convinced of your own convictions. And then you can talk away with real feeling, win hearts, and arrive at your destination without once having to look out of the windows at the boring countryside.

"Oh Rudi." I ignored him.

"Let me tell you, Sophie, that Guy does not do a hand's turn because he *knows* I am going to leave every single penny to him." He looked at me hopefully.

"Well, don't leave it to him."

"I've got no one else to leave it to. Philip already had some money from his mother."

"Ah." Although I no longer cared on any permanent basis, I understood even more plainly that having a little money, Philip had been looking for someone else with a little money to go with it. I could have gone on buying lampshades until doomsday. I felt a start of happiness at the thought of my liberation. I was already so much younger ... almost as young as the schoolgirl and the schoolboy in the car with me. I smiled at Rudi, who promptly frowned petulantly. He wanted an interlocutor; he wanted a battle for the soul of his son. And here I was, *smiling*. He went mumbling on on his own.

"I don't expect gratitude from that boy of mine. But I am not going to stand there and be criticised by a" (he thought for an instant) "Red Indian who goes mooning around in carpet slippers. Do you know he even told me I was washing up the wrong way the other day?"

"But you never *do* any washing-up!"

"I was just washing up a few teacups when he came in and started criticising me. It upset me so much I broke a teacup. And then I set fire to my waste-paper basket. You see what that boy does to me since he got this Jehovah's Witness!"

My mother leant forward obediently as though someone had jerked the strings.

"I believe they take drugs."

"Of course they take drugs," said Rudi, surprised to think anyone should dream that they did not. "There is no question about it. They have orgies, they take drugs, and one day there will be a police raid and Guy will find himself in jail. And do you think that will wake him up?"

"No," said my mother with gratification.

"No!" said Rudi. "He will wake up the day after I am dead. Only then will he understand what it is all about."

He was deeply shaken. The thought of all his furniture, and all his furniture vans, and then his own death, and Guy waking up one morning without him, unable to cope, but at last having a revelation of what it was all about—these images were dramatic enough to make the car journey quite enjoyable.

I had been leaning back placidly in my seat, getting on with the new pleasant task of being myself with no Philip in my thoughts, but these parents were too much for me. I began to feel irritable as though I'd been barked at continuously by a noisy dog.

Rudi was looking straight at me, imploring me to bark back. His expression was like a dying duck's: "Please, please. Kick me. That's all I ask." I said:

"All right. All right! You've got me. You've led me on and goaded me, and now you've got me to answer back—"

"Stuff and nonsense—"

"You've done it deliberately because you're not happy until you've reduced Guy and me to a stupid, squelching, soaking pulp of emotion. Then you can say: 'Oh well, I think they've got some feelings.'"

"If we thought you had some feelings for us that would make all the difference."

"You want to get us down to an animal level. An older brain always wants to subjugate a younger, more active brain than its own, and through emotion drag it down to the bottom of the ditch."

"Sophie!" (My mother)

"Poor Guy. He's just a hunted little old man. He's like a hunted hare."

This was so untrue that I nearly laughed while saying it; but there was *enough* truth in it to stop the play.

In fact the effect was like a thunderbolt. They both became absolutely silent and nodded their marionette heads as though the oracle had spoken. Hitchin drove faster than ever, and we whistled through the lanes.

I thought I ought to go on and consolidate my anger. So I said:

"You want me to deny Mr Ruback, don't you?"

My mother stroked my knee to calm me.

"No, no. Not if—"

"He pulls me out of the mud, and you want me to deny him. That's it, isn't it?"

"My dear Sophie," Rudi began in conciliating tones.

"No. It's too much. You've got no integrity."

I'd earned the right to sit in a disagreeable silence for up to three minutes. Presently Rudi began to hum: te-tum tee-ee tum, te-tum tee-ee tum. At last he was enjoying the outing! He even looked out of the window: "How beautiful! Better than Hampstead Heath, I must say."

Nothing could be seen but a brand-new set of grassy banks.

Until that moment I'd forgotten how much I loved these two children, these two beloved gnomes. But seeing them both swivelling their heads to look out and cry: "How beautiful!" now that they'd had their ration of drama, I understood that they needed emotions which were out of the range of their elderly lives, that they had been spoiled by dramatic youths, and that they must be loved for refusing to give in to age—and for not knowing that they were old in the first place. It was only at that moment I noticed Rudi was wearing what he thought were English tweeds, a kind of sage-green houndstooth, very French. He dressed nearly as badly as Philip. Once when I was walking along Cork Street, Rudi shot out of some tailoring shop with half an overcoat pinned to him, and tried to have a conversation with me about it. "It's got all the colours of the rainbow in it!" he cried. Looking closely at a very ordinary mud-coloured piece of cloth is not aesthetically invigorating; no Englishman today would have been seen dead in it, not loud enough.

"Hampstead Heath?" I said provocatively. "What do you know of Hampstead Heath, Rudi?"

"Why, I walk on it every day. The French Avenue, the Broad Walk, the Lesbians' Bathing Pool …"

Rudi's vision of the Heath was positively invigorating. It was, in his view, covered with attractive women. Every now and then he came on an old man who had just leapt on a young girl and was biting her breasts. Rudi would chase him away with his stick. He was always ready to save a lesbian who got into difficulties in the bathing pool. Rudi said the pool was fourteen feet deep, full of carp and dirty old lilies, and, if you opened your mouth, dusty insects like waterboatmen went flowing in with all their legs.

As we went deeper and deeper into the English countryside, it seemed to change in an effort to fit in with Rudi's conception of it. Continental public houses, almost Swiss chalets, appeared at the roadside. There seemed to be an endless number of pastry-cake shops. In the end we drew up near a Bavarian village, and Rudi said there was an antique shop with an old calf-bound set of Dickens, and was I interested in having it for my flat? (My efforts to do up my flat were well known.) I said I was. In that case, said Rudi, we must put on a little act, as he did with Hitchin. He and I must go in together, and he would try to dissuade me from buying it, in order to keep the price down so that I appeared to be buying it against my will. I said I would prefer it if he did the buying and I did the dissuading, since he knew the price of things so much better than I did. It was agreed. But Rudi seemed unhappy because he said he was used to the opposite role.

Hitchin backed the big car down a lane and kept the engine running. My mother remained inside, looking mysterious and guilty.

Rudi and I then entered the miniature antique shop about as unobtrusively as bullocks forcing their way into Thomas Goode's in South Audley Street. The room inside was so like Willie Broughton's that I was moved. To my horror Rudi went straight up to the books and began to talk in an odd, stilted voice like a schoolmaster repeating a lesson.

"Ho-hum, do I want these books?"

"No, of course you don't," I muttered.

I began to look at some tables with china dishes stacked on them, praying that he would calm down.

"I don't think I want any more books," said Rudi loudly.

"Certainly not." I said it almost bitterly into the opposite corner of the room.

"I've got hundreds and hundreds up at the hall." This was a direct reference to Maddox Hall, his famous old house, which was only a quarter of a mile away. Anyone listening would instantly have doubled the price of everything in the shop.

"You do not want any more. I've told you that." I was extremely sharp with him.

"Don't I?" asked Rudi, puzzled and beginning to take me seriously.

"*No*. For heaven's sake!"

He looked at me anxiously, and returned the book he was holding to the shelf. Then he came over and stood by me. In a deep, draughty whisper he puffed out:

"But I thought you said you wanted them for your flat?"

"Shsh! I *do* want them."

"Well, why didn't you let me buy them then?" He was hissing away just like Guy.

"Shsh! Because you ruined everything by being so obvious."

"Listen, my dear, I have been in this business for forty years," going back to his normal tone, and very offended. "Are you trying to teach me my own business?"

I sighed. "No, Rudi."

The young couple who had been sitting throughout in the gloom at the back of the shop came forward when we had finished our quarrelsome amateur dramatics, and we bought the books from them for ten pounds, which was excessive.

I was about to carry them out, when Rudi made a lordly gesture.

"No, no. They will take them out to the car for us. Won't you?"

It was the final let down.

We all trooped along the lane to the spot where the car, looking larger than ever, stood humming at the ready for a quick get-away. The expensive books were packed away in the boot beside our weekend luggage, while my mother held her head in nun-like reverie inside. Hitchin, in his peaked cap, got out and solemnly locked the boot. Then Rudi climbed back into the car, looking on the whole quite pleased with himself.

"Well?" asked my mother, naturally expecting some story of professional hard bargaining.

Silence. Each of us looked away sulkily in an opposite direction. At last Rudi squirmed uneasily and said:

"You shouldn't have been so *definite*."

"But you told me to dissuade you!"

"Yes, I know. But you see it is normally I who do the dissuading, and then Hitchin buys them. But if I were to put him off like that, he would never dare to buy. I told you we shouldn't have changed roles, because I am so used to being the dissuader I do it automatically." He added: "You have to have an instinct for these things."

I could not laugh, or cry, or divorce him, so I sat there until we pulled into the drive.

There was no colder place, I swear, in the whole of England than Maddox Hall. I have woken up there with my glass of water frozen to my bedside table. None of the windows actually closed, and when changing for a ball in winter you would be warmer outside on the hoar-frost of the lawn than in the bedrooms where the north wind whistled through from end to end, ruffling the silk covers on the beds.

Although my mother's bedroom was next door to mine, she looked anxious, and directly we arrived, started trying to lock herself in. She had stopped flirting with Rudi abruptly at the end of the drive, and started talking about her tapestry work on which she was embroidering some glorious words from the Psalms.

After tea, which was coldish, in front of a fire only just that minute lit and too young to give out heat, we all vanished in different directions. I decided to do a round of the rooms opened to the public to see whether they were worth forty pence. Rudi said he had put some more furniture in them to make them look bigger. In the hall, there was a brace of pheasant flopped across the high polish of the table, and I stopped to look at them. They were the brown that Rudi's new suit was not. The male bird with its cape of red-gold feathers gave off shots of purple iridescence as you moved the soft body. Although the little blue-green head fell about brokenly and piteously at the top of the gold body, it was dressed by life like a piece of Ken Lane jewellery, so sumptuously that your fingers almost became cruel as you admired the flashy brooch it could have made. The she-bird with her moth and tabby-cat wings lay beside it. And I touched them and turned them over, these woodland creatures, so absolutely clean and spotless, in an effort to get to know everything about the sensitive brown depths of the woods.

When I wandered from there into the library and found Rudi sunk gloomily into a chair, I realised he had been there all that time in silence, and that his happiness was much more precarious than I had ever thought. Without moving, he said sombrely:

"What is the use of having children?" He looked at me.

"I'm sorry about those books. I was still thinking about Guy, and I forgot what we were doing."

"So—idiotic—unimportant. You know that."

"Guy will never learn from me. Because he does not think I have anything to give. He underestimates me. He will only learn from me by accident. He prefers to go to strangers with alien thoughts, and worship them. He will let himself be bought with magic and drugs. Instead of coming to his own father who loves him."

A floorboard creaked overhead, pressed by my mother's foot. Were her thoughts of me the same?

Rudi said:

"A child is not a miracle to itself. It is only a miracle to the parents who love it. Consequently those parents will do anything for the child. And the child will do nothing for the parents. The child belongs to the father, but the father does not belong to the child. That is how the terrible situation comes about."

He shook his head.

"I am proud of the fact that I work day and night. But why should I be? It's my wish to work. I believe that you should leave the world a better place than you found it. I have a horror of people who have nothing to do. Or who are *slow*. Or have silly faces ... I work for my son. And when that son comes to me, I drive him away scornfully because he does not work."

That word "work" sent me an involuntary vision of Philip in the past, bent over a desk, patiently writing letters for three-quarters of an hour while waiting for me. Rudi's injustice and favouritism forced me to say:

"Oh Rudi, why do you only ever talk about Guy? What about Philip?"

"Philip? I could never ... ever ... be *certain* about Philip. His mother was so beautiful, and so clever. And so cold."

"Oh don't be so absolutely *ridiculous*, Rudi. He looks like you!"

"Does he?"

"Of course he does. Ask anyone."

"Well, I don't know. Not even Muriel knows." He was so jealous of Philip he was ready to discredit him even to himself.

"My God, Rudi. No wonder he feels so left out, and hardly ever comes up to Hampstead ... If you say this to him, it will *kill* him."

"I have never said it to him. And I will never say it to him."

"Well, don't even think it."

"I cannot guarantee my thoughts, my dear. That is why Philip needs you. Because you make him feel safe, and give him home for his feelings."

"Don't say that! First Pussy, then Willie Broughton, and now you. It's not fair."

"Listen, I educated that boy and brought him up, and all the time I *knew* ... that he did not care tuppence for me."

"So what? Does Guy care tuppence for you?"

"No. I don't know."

"Well then. How do you know Guy is your son?"

"From his lousy stinking behaviour."

Rudi got up, looking deeply depressed, and walked slowly out of the room—like an old man. But he was an old man! An old man playing at being an old man is a dangerous old man. What relentless energy and invention. I remembered what Guy had said to me about him: "Father? He's developed all the mystical qualities, the qualities we're trying to develop at the lectures, *entirely through material means*. He's a keen observer, never misses a thing, he's on the ball every minute of the day, he trusts people, goes out to every new experience like a child, sleeps soundly, never has a day's illness, and is intuitive to the point of second sight. And he's done it all through furniture and women. He's a—*monster*!"

I heard the monster laboriously mounting the central wooden staircase, step by step. Then he crossed the little wooden gallery and stopped. I thought he must have gone along the right-hand corridor into his bedroom because there was dead silence.

After about three minutes I heard his voice in the distance saying something in a reasonable conversational tone. There was no answer. He didn't seem to expect one, because again after a few seconds he started up in exactly the same quiet, persuasive tone—the tone you might put on when arguing with a rather nice wife in order to clear up some minor misunderstanding.

I felt a chill. Rudi, of all people, talking to himself. And so reasonably too. Carrying on a conversation, as though he had put his head into a cupboard and was chatting to a spirit. It was at the same time so natural I felt as if I were doing it myself, and had only just that minute found out. Was it that Rudi lived off his thoughts, then, just as I did? Until they forced their way out through his mouth, and took on a second life? Answered him back in his own voice?

I felt I ought to go up to him and save him from himself. He could talk to me quite freely, and he knew it. Possibly he didn't know what he was doing. He found himself alone, and therefore he dropped into this dialogue with himself. I must go up to him straight away and explain to him what he was doing. If I had caught him trying to walk about on his hands I couldn't have been more upset.

I got as far as the stairs when he started again. This time I could hear it quite clearly.

"I must tell you frankly, I am embarrassed ... to put it plainly ... you are much too good for the job." He stopped and moved his feet. From the sound of his voice I calculated that he must be almost exactly opposite a tall pot of jasmine, just out of the hot-house and in flower, which stood half way down the corridor on a little painted table.

"Both socially," he paused, "and *professionally*," said Rudi with something like triumph in his voice.

I went upstairs, and hailed him gently.

"Are you all right?"

He turned his head.

"Perfectly all right, thank you."

I put on the voice of a nursing sister pecking a difficult patient in order to distract him from what he's doing.

"I'd love to go out and see the animals …"

"Well, help yourself. There are only two ponies left—and look out for Polly if you go in to see her. She coughs like this—"

He splayed out his arms and coughed in a hoarse open-chested way with the whole of his body. It was so exactly like a horse which has been eating green apples and is trying to blow the core and pips out of its chest that I opened my eyes. So Rudi, the metropolitan, the continental, not only understood his animals but could imitate them to perfection.

"That's marvellous! Can you do anything else?"

He looked at me tolerantly, and replied as though *I* were the patient.

"Yes, yes. Winding up the grandfather clock in the hall, owls, pheasant, that little fox terrier Guy used to have. Anything else you want to know?"

"Sorry! But I didn't know you were such a good mimic."

"Of course I am a good mimic. I am good at everything."

I realised that I'd been patronising him, just as Guy patronised him. I tried to patch it up by talking about the fox terrier.

"Was that that beastly little dog with dirty pink whiskers that used to go 'fooph' under the door to get attention?"

"Yes. It went 'fooph' every time you tried to talk. It was disgusting. Where is your mother?"

"Locked in, sewing a sampler."

Rudi looked mischievous.

"Ah. Locked in, is she?" He started creeping along the opposite corridor, just as I had crept about only a moment ago in order to listen in to him. The timber house reported his movements by uttering the sounds of a galleon straining in a gale. When he was opposite my mother's door, he bent down and called through the keyhole freshly:

"Cuckoo!"

There was the noise of someone falling over a foot-stool. Then silence.

"Are you all right?" called Rudi, exactly as I had done to him.

My mother's voice came through, distressed and protesting. It went on for a few sentences and then petered out.

This healthy playfulness, which always seemed part of life at Maddox Hall, was exactly the tonic I needed personally. It stopped me taking myself too seriously. Also there were large pieces of my childhood embedded in different parts of the house. I could go back to the time before I loved Philip; it was reassuring. Philip, who was seven years older than I, was always away when I was here; a grown-up figure at school, and then Cambridge and National Service. After that Europe and the States. I guessed that my mother had been brooding quietly on the past in her room and Rudi had upset her and made her fall over at some moment when she was travelling back in her young thoughts, safe and sound, perhaps making, all over again, on an invisible sewing machine, some invisible clothes for me to go to school in. I felt I must go and talk to her.

But first I ought to clear up Rudi's conversation with the pot of jasmine. So I said:

"By the way, did you know you were talking to yourself in the corridor, just now?"

"Yes, of course."

"Oh."

"I have decided that I shall have to ask Mrs Wynne to leave. And it is not at all easy. Let me tell you that it is much much harder than having a divorce. When you have a divorce you start by having rows and you have an opportunity to work yourself up and get angry. But if you get angry with your housekeeper, she holds her tongue because she is getting paid for it. And you can say what you like, and she won't *budge*." He shuddered. "I could have her with me for life, that's what frightens me. I can't go into the kitchen any longer to get some water for my whisky because I can't stand the way she says 'good evening' to me. It's her slow smiling unlined face that does it." He clutched his head. "It's enough to drive you mad to hear that woman say 'good evening.' You know, I used to be fond of my food, but since she came my wants have got fewer and fewer. In the end I said: 'Just leave me out a light winter salad.' Anything so that she doesn't talk to me. I can't stand the atmosphere. I feel as though my head's splitting. And she always wants something I haven't got, an egg-beater or a lemon-squeezer. Who cares about these things?"

He went away, muttering.

When there was silence again, I rapped gently at my mother's door. She gave her familiar anxious little cough.

"Who is it?"

"Only me, darling."

The wards slid back in the lock: clunk.

My mother had somehow managed to make the inside of that bedroom warm and comfortable. Heaven knows how she had done it. All the bedrooms were peculiar shapes, with tilted floors on which dressing tables stood at unhappy angles. Low, spotted mirrors reflected your stomach. Four-poster beds, as a contrast, were high, and spread out inside was the false top of an alpine meadow. You climbed up the side, the meadow broke under you, and you lowered yourself into a trough or coffin with a hygienic lining of iced linen. Spreading your cold, jointed limbs along the space provided, you stretched out your hand to the antiquated bedside lamp and seized the press-button switch. At once a powerful electric shock—rather like having a lifetime's rheumatism crammed into one second—shot down to your shoulder, leaving your arm like a piece of watered silk. There was a nasty flash, a bang, and deep velvety darkness.

8

My mother had turned on every bar of the electric fire. She was flushed. Her nightdress and dressing-gown, pink clothes, hung over hard, dark chairs of leather with studs on them, concealing them. A pillow from one of the beds had been set into the frame of a low window, keeping out the cold air like a sandbag.

She had been walking to and fro, and had built an atmosphere around herself; deep, sweet, severe, gentle, anxious. She was at her best. It was like being at the secret centre of the woods. I thought of the hen pheasant downstairs.

She began at once:

"So you are going to Normandy? Hmm. It's perfectly all right for a short holiday, but don't stay away too long. How's Philip taken it?"

I was so surprised that I was, so to speak, naked. She was playing the fatal rôle of being my mother.

"*Taken* it? I haven't even told him yet. It's nothing to do with him."

"Oh you must tell him. You owe it to him. You can't just walk out on him without an explanation."

"Look—Don't—I feel as though I'm going mad! It's the way you phrase things. I'm not engaged to him."

"To all intents and purposes."

"No! Stop pushing me and inventing things."

"You were until you went to see that man in Brighton."

"I was *not*."

"I always hoped that you would have been married by now—you're thirty-one, you know—and that I would have had some grandchildren to give me joy. Other women of my age have two or three grandchildren. When Philip came to see me the other day, I noticed he stopped outside to talk to Mrs Wynne's grandchild. And it gave me a pang."

"It gave *you* a pang!"

"Nobody can understand what's holding things up between you two."

I could feel that my face was as much an electric fire as the one on the floor. I made a movement towards the door. My mother said sadly:

"Don't shut me out of your life."

I stood there with the strength dripping out of the soles of my feet, trapped and sullen. I knew perfectly well that talking about a problem to my mother always made it a hundred times worse. At last I said in a thick, odd voice, making the same prodigious effort that mentally defective people do to get words out:

"I haven't ... *got* a life at the moment. But if you'd just let me go away and make one ..."

"Oh darling." She came towards me on the edge of tears, and wanted to embrace me and suck me under.

"Don't touch me!"

"What's the matter now?"

I made clumsy protective gestures for myself to match my voice. I was already reduced and disgraced, and found a sort of illiterate, emotional swill in my head. My eyes were on the ground. I knew that if she tried to touch me, or *hold* me, I should either pass into a kind of epileptic trance, feign death, and turn myself into a lump of brute flesh, or else strike the beloved hands away.

She was so pretty, small, and distraught. I longed to comfort her, but I could not bear the emotional level which seemed to be her natural ground for communicating on subjects of importance. I loathed the reduction of the human being—the dripping hot tears that burnt you down like a candle stump—that appeared to be necessary as a prelude to a conversation about realities. How I longed to be able to say to her: "You don't do it that way. You discuss something impersonal, and while you're doing so, you put out one tentacle and then another, and so on, until some information has gone over to the other side without too much emotional damage. You use an impersonal subject to mop up the thunder and lightning."

She was upset, turned her head to one side, and began to tremble.

"I don't understand you. You're not my daughter any more. A strange creature has taken her place. A woman with a heart of stone. Why can't I have a normal daughter I can talk to sometimes?"

I made another supreme effort to choke down my disgust, at myself, at the scene, and at her. This disgust of mine was masculine and the result of taking care of her for so many formative years. What she was asking was perfectly reasonable. All I had to do was to stop behaving like a lunatic.

Sensing that I had become fractionally more logical, she pressed on:

"You've changed so much lately. You can't see it yourself, but I can. In the car coming down we were quite afraid of you."

"I'm sorry. But you keep getting at me."

"I never say a word to you. Because you can't be spoken to. Look at you now!"

She seemed to be able to recover herself so much more rapidly than I could. There was a split second's recuperation, and then her nerves were all ready for a fresh attack—almost as though this was exactly what they needed to function properly, and they *had* to obtain it for themselves. And she had a way of breathing deeply which quickly revitalised her system with fresh oxygen. Whereas I had the greatest difficulty in breathing at all, or in fact in standing upright and carrying out my part. Another grotesque disadvantage was that I could never think of anything to say.

My mother said:

"I don't know how many more years I've got to live, but I'd like to see you happily married before I die. It's my dearest wish. That is why I can't believe these lectures you go to are any good for you. Because they are taking you away from Philip. And from your mother."

"But that's not true! Just because I've discovered that I'm an idiot, and that the ordinary people at the lectures have more wisdom, and always have had more than I have—"

"Well—"

"This teaching is—more important than my present life. More important than Philip. It frees me—from the necessity of having children—and—conforming to the European pattern."

"And what is this famous teaching?"

"I suppose you'd call it—self-development."

As though my answer was almost incomprehensible, she screwed up her eyes.

"I've never heard of anything so selfish!"

We had arrived at the very centre of her attitudes and values, and they set hard at that instant. Or were they not hardened by the thoughts that Biddy Horner had recently placed in juxtaposition to them? My mother was so vulnerable to those who talked to her about her "rights" and who told her about the duties that were owed to her as a mother. But she also knew in her heart that to play such a rôle after all that had passed between us over the years was a breach of faith; it would no longer hold water. If I sat down and waited, she would shortly respond to the actual relationship between us, the stranger in her mind would be ejected, and we would begin to laugh together as before.

Unfortunately I was on edge. My life was at stake; and I no longer wanted to make allowances for her or to be charmed by her. I was, in turn, playing the daughter, and pressing for moral support and understanding. But having left her abruptly to get on with her own life in the past as best she could, and told her not to interfere with mine, I had no more right to turn round and ask for these things than she had to ask for grandchildren. We were both trying to draw cheques on an empty bank.

And so it was written into our lives that we would always let one another down. And we were doing it at that very moment.

Whenever she allowed her emotions to run wild, and sprang them on me like this, I would behave atrociously and enter a panic condition in which I simply wanted to bang my head against a wall like an animal. I knew the causes. I was terrified that I would have to take on the old psychological burden of being her husband, and adoring her at the same high rate of adoration I had been able to sustain as a child. If I did so, I would lose myself forever. I would wear the clothes she made for me, the life she made for me. I would be forever the dog dressed-up for charades, moving clumsily over the floor in some kind of crocheted shawl, some kind of skirt, that hobbles it and takes away its dignity. The dog which is sentimental and loving, and allows itself to be dressed-up, because it cannot help itself. And while everyone shouts with laughter, it becomes half demented, or tries to die and turns itself into a piece of wood. When I saw this coming ... my reason collapsed and I went mad.

I was now sure that nothing said after this point could pierce so deeply, and I thought that although we still talked we had already finished the conversation. In some ways I began to relax. My mother said repetitiously:

"I've given you twenty years of my life. And I have a right to expect something in return."

I moved the block of stone to one side in my mind.

"Darling, you never said these things before you became so friendly with Biddy Horner ... Wasn't I looking after you all those years?"

"Don't be so absurd. You were a little child."

One of us trembled with injustice, and the other with ingratitude. I wanted to be allowed to leave the room, but conversations and rows with my mother had a way of being diabolically interesting. Part of the trouble was that she was an extremely absorbing woman. Once you had got used to the appalling emotional conditions inside yourself, you remained to observe the source of energy. It was like standing too close to a fire, not because you were cold, but because it was alive. I remained with my arms at my sides, taciturn. I thought the worst was over.

She walked a few more paces, picked up her little black suede gloves and pulled the crumpled fingers through her closed hand to straighten them out. The undersides of the fingers were shiny. As she watched herself perform this task, she said decisively:

"Very well. I shall speak to Philip myself."

"You'll *what*?"

She had suddenly become terrible, with terrible little lips

uttering insane sentences. This bombshell stepped up the pace of things in an instant. I flew at her.

"How dare you interfere! You must be out of your mind. He'll take—you—to—pieces."

She uttered a mocking explosion of breath.

"*He* will? My dear child, I've known Philip since he was a little baby in arms. He doesn't frighten me."

She had got so into the habit of living through me that she saw nothing immoral in taking part in my life. By removing myself to Normandy and studying mysticism, I was denying her a life. She was afraid that I would leave her behind. And so she wanted to marry Philip for me, and obtain the grandchildren to whom she was entitled. In a panting, hysterical voice—I wanted to scream at her but I hadn't the breath for it—I said:

"If you say one word to Philip, I'll never speak to you again as long as I live."

I was so convulsed with rage that I had her attention for an instant. But she looked away back at her gloves.

"You can't blackmail me, my dear," she said bitterly. "You've got no father to protect you. It's my duty to speak."

I shouted straight at her, like a blow aimed out of the centre of my body:

"*That's enough!*"

Quite suddenly she collapsed, fell into a chair and covered her face. She said in quite a different voice, exhausted, strained and quivering:

"I can't stand the worry. You're killing me."

"Oh my God!"

She had turned the tables, and put me into the position of the enraged torturer looking down on the victim. In an undertone, still seething, I muttered: "Take your medicine, can't you?"

She merely repeated:

"I can't stand it. I can't stand it."

I began to walk towards the door, and she pulled herself together. In a shaking voice she tried to reconstruct some sort of bridge between us; she forced herself to see my point of view, and although she sobbed, she was not entirely miserable because she could see those much-prized tears—signs that I had a heart—wet on my face.

"Forgive me! You should be able to talk to your own mother. You know I only have your well-being and happiness at heart. It's so hard to know what to do for the best. And you don't confide in me."

"I don't want to worry you."

She took her hands away from her face, and looked terribly relieved.

"But that's just where you're wrong. I worry when you don't tell me things. It's when you store things up that it worries me so."

"Well, there's nothing to tell you really …"

"What did the man in Brighton say to you that had such an effect on you?" How quick she was; clear bright eyes wide open and the little head held up to listen.

"He just said: 'Don't have anything to do with him,' meaning Philip. He said if I married him, in one week I would be in the attic and he would be in the cellar."

"But how does he *know*?"

"He concentrates. He sees pictures."

"Did he say anything else?"

"Not much. Just said he would never be any good to any woman."

"But that's absolutely ridiculous!"

"Is it? … Well, what about Rudi?"

She was silent. My blow was so shrewd that I was almost

able to smile at her, and there was no need to repeat the often-repeated: "Why don't you marry Rudi?" I said:

"You see, it cuts both ways."

"There's no comparison. I'm coming to the end of my life. And I want to enjoy this last little bit that's left to me."

For the first time she moved me on her own account.

"And you shall, darling. It'll be the best bit of all."

At this she looked so hopeful and pathetic it wrung my heart. There was too much of the visionary in her; when her eyes shone like that it was because they were star-gazing. And it was up to me to fulfil these multifold visions of hers. Another burden to bow me to the ground. With her new hope was born that impulsive goodwill and urge to comprehend my mind that had so often astonished me in the past. It always occurred, as now, after the blackest moments when she had intractably closed all doors to me, and behaved like a vixen. Suddenly: *light*. And when my mother entered into my plans and ideas there was no one like her. She could seize on the potential of the smallest detail, and inspire a whole new area of my mind, to the point of bringing into being images, joys, capacities, I could never have developed on my own. There was a level of excitement, as high as the level of dramatic dialogue had been low, which I have never been able to find in the company of any other human being. On that level you are understood and appreciated in a way that makes you drunk.

And so there was this willingness to try again with me, and to see what it would bring in.

In my turn, I looked at her in a new way. I saw that she was generously giving to me the one thing no one gave to her: safety. Whatever I said or did, I was safe here. Even in the middle of the vilest quarrel I was *at home*. But there was no one who could provide that safety for her. All I had to do was to give her some small pieces of myself, because she had nothing else to hang on to. I was also wise enough to know that I must try to disarm her of that weapon she had discovered when she said: "I shall speak to Philip myself." So I talked to please her and to protect myself.

I told her all about the unsatisfactory side of Philip. The fact that we never quarrelled, that I never spoke my mind, and did not feel fulfilled, but that on the contrary I was being dragged along too fast, and never arrived anywhere or achieved anything. She listened with the greatest interest. At the end of it she gave a resigned sigh and said:

"It's been a strain on me too, you know. Because I knew what you were going through. I only hope I don't break down and blurt things out if it gets too much for me."

She was reminding me of her weapon, and giving herself a loophole for some future piece of misguided behaviour.

I felt dizzy, and my heart was in my mouth again. But you have no power to stop another human being's tongue, except by binding and gagging them and throwing them into a pit. And I was already beginning to get used to the ignominy of the idea; the real horror of it lay in the fact that it would give Philip an opportunity to snub my mother, and he was capable of taking that opportunity.

I saw clearly that if I appealed to her, it would make it seem to be a matter of the first importance, and therefore irresistible. And therefore she would do it. Whereas if I passed it off, I could de-fuse the bomb. I said merely:

"Don't do impossible things."

We had been talking for such a long time in that bedroom with the oak beams, that we had made it our own, and forgotten where we were.

There was the sound of a gong beating far away in the distance. This pleasant muted booming, felt through its vibrations rather than heard, was voluptuously filling the whole house to the brim, filtering up the back staircases and along cold, faraway corridors. Boom. Boom. Boom.

My mother jumped up.

"Well, that's that," she said cheerfully, closing the chapter. And ran to the dressing-table. She powdered all over her face with vigour. As a final concession to sentiment she said talkatively over her shoulder through the powder: "What a pity you don't love him."

"Oh but I do! Very much indeed."

"Well!" And then all ready for some repartee with Rudi at dinner, she said skittishly: "You could have fooled me."

* * *

I could remember right back to the days at Maddox Hall when Rudi had been married to Biddy. Then there were dogs about to keep the hall warm, and you could never get on with anything because there was always so much bustle. There were secret conversations going on all over the house, and people kept changing friends. We each had our own method of getting time to ourselves. Guy at eleven would play "Chopsticks" in the downstairs playroom until he had driven everyone away. I would loiter with a book in the long corridor to the west wing where no one ever went because it was hung with gloomy nudes. These nudes were cut up pieces of the same human body; a girl with ginger hair. Arms, legs, torsos, breasts, all well-painted, and each one of them signed by a few strokes of ginger hair. If they had been a little less well-painted, you wouldn't have bothered to stop and look at them. But they were so good that you stared at them, and by the end of the corridor you knew that girl physically better than her lover could have done in the same amount of time.

But she was gloomy. Being nude meant nothing to her. I don't think she even knew she *was* nude; she wasn't modest, she wasn't erotic, she was an artist's model sitting at ten shillings an hour day after day without a stitch on. And she kept everyone away from that part of the house while she did it.

The advantage was that you could get on with your book. The great sin in those days was to be "found reading," or even to be "found" at all. You were supposed to be downstairs taking part in the merry, active life of the house. It was perfectly all right to read in the sitting-room in front of the fire because then you could be interrupted and interrogated. It was always Biddy who did the finding. "So here you are!" she'd call out. "Aren't you coming downstairs? It's so cold up here." It was freezing up there. And ghostly. All the old chimneys had starlings' nests where the wind rustled. Going to the lavatory after dark was terrifying. I made a practice of groping along the corridor with my eyes closed in case I saw something; until someone told me that you could see them *much better* with your eyes closed. If you looked out of the low windows at night there were frozen lawns stretching away and moonlight as coarse as cabbage. It was always perfectly still outside. The gravel paths stood out, with a shadow along one side, and the separate grains of stone could be clearly seen.

Yes, and in the evenings, when you went downstairs, it was a house in which people lost their rings. Rings were taken off the whole time and put down while someone did a filthy chore connected with the dogs or the fire, or the kitchen, or washing hands. The ring then rolled into a crack four hundred years old, and Guy would have to come with a coffee spoon or a pickle fork and look for it. In those cracks you smelt the particular smell of old dirt, which smells sweetish like parsnips cooking, with their odour of urine, sweets, and scent, and is a rich substance hanging together like loam. Guy would always find something else. Sometimes it was a clue from a past treasure-hunt which had been put back in exactly the same place for the next person to find: "Look where muslin tells its beads/Tum-te-tum my next clue reads." Or some such drivel.

This was a reference to Biddy's iron rule in the kitchens. All milk jugs containing milk, buttermilk, cream, or custard (ugh) had limp muslin covers on them, and the muslin was edged with glass beads to hold it in position. When you lifted one of these, the beads hit out at the cold musical sides of the jug. In that larder, where everything was stone—and earth-cold, you could see in those days two or three half-eaten pies lying on the marble shelf—under the pie-crust the piece of dog-china that originally supported the elastic structure would have fallen on its side into a stoup of green gooseberry juice. Beside it would be the wet purple body of a summer pudding. And next to that a rice pudding which had been lifted, still breathing, from the oven with its speckled lung of blistered skin. You could inhale these works of art for as long as you could stand the temperature in there; or until Biddy found you. But nowadays larders and sculleries were forbidden territory.

The last stronghold of childhood was the garden room, where the flowers were done, and mud-caked gardening overalls were hung up. There was an upright telephone on a shelf behind the overalls; it connected you to London and the earpiece was green with age and formed in the shape of a dog's rubber bone. In the large clean wash-basin with its polished brass taps, almost as tall as the telephone, there were some pieces of soap.

Now these soap pieces gave out a smell of exquisite

freshness. I never found out what kind of soap it was. But on a summer day you ran in from the garden and picked them up, cold fragrant slices of milk, and let the hot water flow over them to make foam … and you slowed down, somnambulist, with the pure aromatic steam in your nostrils, and washed away your childhood in movements older than the house, while your own reflection looked at you soapily from the mirror above: "Yes, here I am. You. That's your face. No expression. Just a pudding and a steady pair of eyes. Very primitive. You're growing up. You can't hang about here, washing your hands you know. Quickly, wake up; on to the next bit of your life, the real bit. Off you go. Try not to be an idiot. And good luck, Silly."

But I didn't actually lose my childhood until those famous words were spoken to me in the hotel room.

Until that moment I had been sure of everything. And I had the impression that if I really wanted something, it would be given to me. Now I wasn't sure of anything, and had to reinvest objects and actions with virtue by an act of will.

How curious that Philip had grown up at that basin and gazed into that mirror. It was logical that when my mother arrived down here, and the old memories reasserted themselves, she would have visions of Philip and myself … and she would want to hurry us up. And so she suddenly put the pistol of her age, her hopes and her fears to my forehead.

But far from wanting to give her grandchildren, she had planted in me the desire never to have any children at all. There was the probability that I would revert to type. *I* would become the mother in the bedroom hung with pink gowns. I would harass some unhappy little creature, knead it, blackmail it, appeal to it, and wait for the tears which would tell me that it was still *mine*. *I* would learn to mount the first tread of a stair in a way that would make that child feel it had failed me. Oh yes, I would infallibly learn how to climb stairs.

My violent reaction against this "talk" with my mother took me by surprise. I ran away from it mentally. I was certain that that kind of emotion left behind a form of wet-rot in the brain that contaminated mental action for months ahead. I longed for dry-as-dust conversations with clerks in the mortgage departments of building societies, a season in the Middle East brushing the dust off some comparatively valueless antiquities with a paintbrush, or Caesar's *Gallic Wars* in vile italics.

When Biddy had her way at Maddox Hall, talks like this were going on all over the house. She invited people to follow their most primitive instincts. This was one of the reasons why Philip and Guy couldn't come down without turning yellow and getting violent indigestion; the old associations were too strong for them.

Biddy had a habit of watching you intently while you were reading a book. You would read on against it, until it became too much for you, when you would look up sharply, irritably, to catch her at it. She would then smile at you *and go on staring*. The advantage of a stare is that you can rest inside it; it's a form of protection.

Like so many pretty women, she knew nothing about clothes at all. But she knew that she ought to get herself up on certain occasions. I remember one Christmas she appeared wearing a white crepe blouse with no sleeves and beads sewn on the front like a Marseilles blue film manageress. All she needed was a little torch to show people to their seats. She had gone into a shop in Oxford Street and told them she wanted something smart. I believe it took her less than ten minutes to buy a new dress.

Rudi was horrified. He spent those years doing up the public rooms and threw himself into the task. He brought in panelled Tudor Gothic chairs, draw-top tables, and colossal beds with heavy wooden canopies, all carved and lumpy. Fine tapestries were mended and hung. The floors all had to be polished, and the house never stopped creaking and groaning as though it was in pain. He wrote up the guide book. Mrs Wynne appeared on the scene; and from then on there was always someone polishing, repairing, inspecting, and the house was less lived in. It began to be taken over by something called "the public" or "Rudi's public." Sometimes Rudi went among the public, anonymously, to study their preferences. There was a strong reaction against this foreign-looking man who had come sightseeing alone, perhaps in the hope of picking up some woman. Decent people moved away from him instinctively and spoke in whispers. They disapproved of the way he hurried through the rooms like a, well ... like a noisy vandal. Everyone knew that the proper way to do things was to walk with slowly dragging feet and to show a respect for history by murmuring with pleasure every time one saw a plate, or a picture, or a pot. If you saw a whole chair, you would have to stop and stand still for a moment. If you saw a whole bed with Tudor roses on it, you might have to sit down until you came to yourself again.

One day Rudi put out his hand to straighten a Holbein drawing which had slewed itself to one side, and one of the public took his hand away and said firmly: "Er—I don't think we should touch those." Rudi returned to the hall and took a handful of silver out of the takings to cheer himself up. I don't know whether anyone saw him do it.

He couldn't give up Maddox Hall, which was by now more or less his own creation. And although there were lean bachelor days with nothing but smoked salmon and cake in the larder, he filled the gaps by inviting down women who were full of life, and rather like Biddy. Women who were able to play Plump Mistress of the Household and Intrigue for a weekend, and vanish on Monday morning when he said abracadabra.

By the time Hitchin drove us back to London early on Monday, we were all very ill. We hardly spoke and wanted to get away from one another as quickly as possible. Things improved directly we found ourselves among buildings again. Rudi began to look out of the window. I remembered that I had some Alka-Seltzer in the bathroom cupboard of my flat. My mother, who was talk-drunk after her scene with me and endless exchanges with Rudi, was only able to bring out an occasional phrase: "To him that hath shall be given ..." down to "... *seemeth* to have" and "Time and tide wait for no man," looking at me. Otherwise she had run into the sand, and needed Biddy.

We pulled up outside Rudi's house.

One of his furniture vans was parked there, and the ramp was down at the back of it. Three men were carrying Pussy's yellow chesterfield along the path of Rudi's garden; their feet scuffed on the stone. When they saw him, they put it down and panted.

Rudi got out with a strange look on his face. He hurried up to the men and started giving orders: "Be careful of the feet! They're not strong. Up on the first floor. You'll have to turn it on its side."

It disappeared inside the front door, and Rudi after it. How acquisitive he was.

Later, Hitchin carried the books up to my flat. When I opened the door the first thing I saw on the doormat was a letter from Philip, as white as his flesh. The present! How strong and real the present was, after a weekend in the past. So it was still "on," my love affair. Clocks started to tick in the room. I was aware of where the telephone stood, and that it was part of me.

Hitchin started to talk. He said:

"Old father Hitchin says it's a shame taking it away from the old lady."

"What? Oh yes."

I began to open the letter; at the same time I was thinking that I'd better take a rug with me to Normandy, because it was bound to be cold.

9

Alençon is a day's journey if you leave London on the old ten-thirty train from Victoria, change at Paris in the afternoon, and get a provincial train filled with farmers and dried-up women with shiny unclever black eyes.

In winter the French landscape is covered by sheets and sheets of still water. It is permanently flooded.

I was there before dark, and got out stiffly onto the platform with very little grace, surrounded by France, French talk, French plants and cold French weather. I hadn't the slightest idea who would be there to meet me. The last thing Pussy said was: "I phoned them. They'll be on the platform."

There wasn't a soul on the platform. The wind fitted my coat against me almost to the bone. I stood stock-still beside my two metropolitan suitcases, which looked theatrical, as smart as paint, and rested on golden toenails. But there is a limit to the amount of time you can pass on a platform after having arrived somewhere. I felt gloomy and despondent after a minute, and had to take action.

I picked up the heavy cases, and carried them down to the exit. The long, gritty platform tired me, and those cases were as heavy as corpses and set up a galumphing rhythm of their own.

On the other side of the barrier, standing as still as I had been standing on the platform, were four children as arrogant as tiger-lilies. All were dressed identically in navy-blue wool. One was female and had plaits. With them, also rock-still, was a spaniel which had just come out of a tin of golden syrup.

I promptly put down my suitcases.

We observed one another with the calm indifference of rival species. I hadn't spent the summers at Maddox Hall for nothing. I knew how to slide in a blank country stare over my eyes. It was Wiltshire against Sarthe. The supercilious bright red mouth, the eyes as pitiless as a sheet of floodwater, the bramble-scratched limbs impervious and strong as rubber.

Seconds later a woman of about my own age came up and broke the spell over them, so that they fell into life. It was, I knew it would be, Iris de Salignac.

These strong, India-rubber children closed in around me, and they remained so from that moment and throughout my visit. From being the lonely traveller, the tutor on the platform, eaten by the wind, I was instantaneously at the centre of life.

We all got into a corrugated iron car and slammed the tin doors. The children talked courteously. Iris told me their names: François, Yolaine, Pierre, Tanguy. The dog was called Aiöu.

We shot away across the countryside. It was flat. Iris pointed out the landmarks; as she did so the children looked for me in this or that direction, in case I should not know exactly where to look. They were highly intelligent, but they had the absolute simplicity of those who are close to their origins and whose origins are clear water.

The château was called St Emilion, and was on the other side of the village of St Emilion.

There was a small moat, more of a stone ditch really, and

a lodge where four more children and a dog were playing on a patch of earth which had been beaten until it shone. The contrast between the two sets of children and the dog was alarming, becase the lodge children were scrawny, and the dog was a thin freckled animal which took up craven attitudes.

No one seemed in the least bit put out by the difference. The lodge children smiled, the dog fawned, and we drove on.

The château was deceptive, because it hadn't looked so big in the photograph. But when you got up to it you saw that the proportions were very large. The front door was a great Norman arch which opened in two halves. Sitting on the steps in front of it was a fifth navy-blue child, which was greeted with shouts of joy from the car. This child, which was playing with an enormous cardboard box, got up to receive us. It was perhaps about two years old, and appeared to be alone and in sole charge of the house.

"That's Jean," said Iris. "He has to stay behind because he's the baby."

The children took me to my room. There was a wooden staircase which went up in a gigantic curve quite bad enough to give you vertigo near the top. In England it would have been banned to children and locked off with a gate. I went up with extreme caution. These children climbed it laboriously all day long; and Jean was left behind to pull himself up without a sound of complaint, after all the others had gone ahead. Normally they would return and pass him, half way up, as they went down again. Whereupon he would turn round and begin the descent, again in silence.

We all pelted down the corridor, laughing out loud as though it was the best thing in the world to run down a corridor. François flung open the door of my room. It was entirely panelled and carved from floor to ceiling. Along the beams in the ceiling were painted coats of arms and the *fleur-de-lys*. The children pointed out the bullet-holes made by the Germans.

There was a four-poster bed elegantly hung with what looked like fine white and yellow linen, but which turned out to be fine plastic. A little tapestry *chauffeuse*. A cupboard you could have got an elephant into, with hinges that whined like old women. A beautiful stone balcony in front of long tightly-closed windows. There was no heating whatsoever. I felt perfectly at home.

Henri de Salignac appeared, carrying my suitcases. He said he was Scottish, and would see me at dinner. He shooed the children out of the room, and shut the door to give me a moment's privacy.

I found a door in a corner of the room, set above three steps. I opened it and discovered that a half-size bath and a basin had been crammed in, cemented in, to form one of those famous continental bathrooms which start out about the size of an ordinary lavatory and gradually expand as unimaginable half-size bathroom furniture is homogeneously chocked into them. I washed, sniffed the soap (out of habit) and put out the electric light. The switch was in the form of a miniature propeller which you turned sideways. The casing of the switch had been gnawed away at one point; I could see some silver wire inside which vibrated.

All the electric light bulbs were about twenty feet up and dark gold in colour.

By the time I went down to dinner, the children had put themselves to bed, with the exception of François. They did this every night as soon as there was no more light in the sky. The intense, struggling bodies simply laid themselves down, absolutely worn out, and the life of all four of them changed into a communal dream. François seemed to want to join the dream, and to know he was missing something important that the others were doing, because his head nodded and he excused himself before the meal was over.

We ate at a circular grey marble table in the big centre room. There was an especially sharp knife, rather like a Prestige kitchen knife, which you kept beside you for the whole meal resting the blade on a silver cross-bar.

A great deal of bread was eaten. It was wise not to let your diagonal cuts of bread stray down too close to the edge of the marble table. Aiöu, who was extremely fond of bread, and I believe subsisted entirely on it, would come up and take it gracefully. It's true, there was the noise of champing jaws afterwards, but the deed itself was done as perfectly as a cricketer taking a catch, just a silky lifting movement, made as though in slow motion inside limitless time. He was lightly applauded, and you were thought to have been careless.

Aiöu was a golden snob with perfect manners. His main job in life was to play with the children, and to set value on different parts of the château and the grounds outside. His peak position was in the little blue salon after dinner in front of the fire: there he was humble and playful, almost a puppy again, and had golden thoughts. In the dining-room he was a fraction more guarded: there was food about, he had certain rights in the open hearth of the large marble fireplace, and servants who went to and fro had to be watched. Out on the terrace at the back, where there were painted chairs set about in the sun, he at once became a noble animal, just like one of the stone lions, and definitely on duty. Anywhere else in the grounds, he was alert, bristling, careful, and, if necessary, ferocious. His manners towards the children were so excellent that they were a study in what love and tolerance in a nanny should be. He never went near the lodge dog, or spoke to the servants, or skulked near the kitchens. The invisible plans of the territories which he had divided up in order of their importance were not for a second confused in his mind. As he trotted from one to another, from safety to danger, his body underwent physiological changes, his ruff stiffened as though it had just had a volt of electricity combed through it, and his head rode two inches higher.

That first night, we sat in the blue salon for about twenty minutes before going to bed. There was a television set and we watched two shadow men boxed in and interviewing one another to the point where they became one. The two shadows in the French box continued to do this throughout my visit, and are no doubt doing it at this very minute. But they had to compete with the enormous dark château and the cubic depth and silence of the night that covered us.

For miles and miles in every direction there was nothing; cold fields, a few lanes, some flat streams, every inch of it covered with this black air. You could have heard a dry branch crack at least half a mile away. There was not a soul, not a sound.

I went up to bed. This meant finding my way through three salons that were intercommunicating, and pulling open huge doors heavy with moulding in the pitch dark. The perilous stairs glimmered at me under one of those fading gold bulbs. I noticed a flat wrought-iron bar had been fastened across the inside of the front doors. No getting in or out.

How I missed the children as I climbed the staircase. Another long dark corridor, and there was the safety of my room. I'd put out some photographs, and books, and sheets of writing paper. I looked with a friendly eye on these simple objects. It was so cold that at first I wasn't sure how I was going to be able to undress. Then I remembered the way it had been done at school. You got into bed and built a kind of pie of sheets and blankets; inside this, shuddering with the agony of it, you got one layer off over your head and pulled on the next layer. There was a moment when a strip of your back was exposed, and then the thing was done, and you had to radiate heat in order to warm up your night-clothes.

I got on with the job, sitting in the middle of my pie, in the middle of the four-poster. One thing was certain; it was no good being afraid of ghosts, having a heart-attack, or simply calling out "Help!" I was totally isolated at the end of cold dark corridors at the centre of a cold dark house, somewhere in France. Once this was established, I set about the ancient rites which animals develop in order to stay alive. These consist in warming up your accommodation by running inside it while lying down, then turning over and over until you have generated enough heat to go to sleep, and so worn yourself out that however you lie it's comfortable.

I took a curious pleasure in the fact that there was plenty of time in which to do these things. That was a feature of life at St Emilion; there was endless time. You could go into a great room and take as much as you wanted. The rooms were full of it, and it went back to medieval days, and back again to prehistoric days.

The last thing I remembered before going to sleep was that my feet were so cold and so far away that unless I slept in a circle, bringing my knees up to my chin, I would never, never, thaw them out ... I had the sensation of tripping and missing a step, and gave a jump ...

... I opened my eyes.

There were five cherubs and a dog posted around my bed like silent sentries. They looked into my face as though it was the much-desired toy of childhood, and I looked at them and could not remember a time when waking up had not been a beautific moment. I stretched out my arms to them; they crowed with joy, held me with cucumber-cold hands and made romping movements along the edge of the bed. Aiöu made corresponding noises and gestures, (slightly ridiculous in a cocker spaniel). Their voices came out of tiny white teeth, and were as high and clear as bells. When they had examined my nightdress, run their fingers along the edges of my books, gently lifted up and put down my jar of cold cream, all at the highest pitch of excitement, they seemed suddenly to sense a voice calling them from outside in the gardens because they said goodbye all at once and ran away, exhilarated by what they had seen. I heard them in the far distance descending those terrible stairs. I guessed it would take Jean ten minutes to get down them.

A young girl, Christine, brought me a boiled egg, coffee and bread on a tray. She seemed to be not much older than the children.

And so I ate my first breakfast in Normandy, lifting freezing fingers out of my bed, and biting into every fragment of toast and spoonful of egg as though I had never eaten such godlike food before. I can taste it now, that first simple breakfast of brown toast, and I can feel the hot dome of the solid brown egg sitting in the silver egg cup. I had time to shake coarse white salt over it and to taste the grains as they melted on my tongue.

I generated long-lasting tranquil thoughts. They hung almost motionless in my mind, and were perfectly empty but for the light they gave out.

At last I got up and dressed, and looked out of the window to where play was going on down below in the walk around the house. This walk was covered with grey pebbles as hard as obsidian. If you broke one open, it had a blue eye inside it, surrounded by white, like the yolk of an egg.

The children had some cardboard boxes as large as themselves. They got inside these and ran about with only their feet showing, bumping into one another and calling out: "*Bonjour!*" I suppose it was a form of jousting. It was exceedingly funny.

There were no newspapers, so every morning I read the *Le Monde* I had brought with me. A paragraph of this dry black rhetoric taken once a morning, like a concentrated biscuit of current affairs for astronauts and others in some eternal dimension outside civilisation, was exactly the amount required for good health. It maintained discipline, and checked a tendency to grin at nothing. I never had the sensation that what I was reading was old news; I have always felt that everything that has or will happen is going on all the time, and it's entirely up to you when you tune in to it.

No description of life on the first floor at St Emilion is real without a brief drawing of the lavatory. The one I got to know was entered through a wallpapered door, and locked from within by a tiny bolt that trembled on its screws. Once you had got yourself used to the gloom, you saw you were in yet another brown corridor but with narrow flimsy walls and a ceiling lost in the gods. At the far end of this, in a turret, was an enormous china conch-shell, on which a wooden horseshoe, having been clamped down but never actually fixed, had an unsatisfactory floating action. A slit window, suitable for shooting arrows through, lit this from twenty feet above. From those heights a chain of great length hung down and could be caught as it swayed in the draughty, rumbling wind that used this tunnel as the most direct means of getting across the building from one side to another. When the wind blew, it stirred languid green cobwebs built some hundreds of years ago and now carrying a heavy load of assorted trivia which it was never originally intended they should bear. And the same dry brown leaf rustled its way along the floor every day, scratching with the tips of its withered glove. Suddenly: bump! One of the children had arrived at the door in a hurry and found it locked. In whatever shell-shocked attitude this caught you, you were wise to hurry up and to give up philosophising, since the cannonade had only just begun. *Bump!* A second charge far more determined than the first. The cobwebs floated overhead, the chain swung, the wind lifted the brown leaf and threw it against the door, while the damnable horseshoe swung wide, lost contact with the base and fell to the ground with a clatter.

Every day the same whitish-grey sky enclosed our world. The black branches of the trees went through it. Sometimes there were ice clouds, gross and hard as cheap lard. You waited for hailstones or sheets of glass to come crashing down. But the sky very rarely moved; it only thickened and grew colder. The children were put out scorched and radiant, over the touchy ground.

Every evening a mist, a white hand trailing a white chiffon scarf, approached the château and wrapped it up for the night. No dogs were ever left out: Aiöu slept with the children.

I passed ideal days. I gave to everything I did a rapt attention. When I went for a walk, a serene, silent wash of time hypnotised me and took away all burdens. I listened, with the children, at telegraph poles. Inside the barrel was a choir, a descant, a hive of bees burying their music; some were louder than others, and thrummed energetically. But

I preferred the ones as delicate as musical boxes. These harmonious objects, set quivering in Paris, played quietly to themselves and were there for you to listen in to whenever you wanted.

From all this peace, came a new development of spirit and sensibility. If that modern hotel room had been built to coarsen us spiritually, then St Emilion was the antidote. I had found out that I could only arrive somewhere by slowing down.

But the postman began to bring me letters.

This old man, who wore steel glasses, bicycled up once a day across the obsidian pebbles with a canvas satchel containing a white love letter from Philip. Each letter ended with the words: "Love me? I love you."

Falling into this silent pool, they began to work on me. Facts became hazy at the edges, our dissimilarities no longer seemed of the slightest importance. There was plenty of space here to absorb any number of awkward characteristics. They would be mopped up in seconds. We were all of us at St Emilion self-reliant, separate people. Another thing: you hardly ever used money here, or saw it out in the open where it always looked raw, like pieces of meat.

One day I decided to walk into the woods at the back because the sun had come out: an extraordinary occurrence! I approached the still centre, going along a springy mattress of dried-out leaves. There was a gap in the trees overhead, and I found I had got into a warm blond hole of light. The air was scented like barley sugar. I was so happy I looked instinctively for Philip.

I sent my mind back to him. It came over me with absolutely total force: *I want him.* And he is waiting for me and loves me. I want that milky brow with the cross lines on it, lightly corrugated, the brow that I have sipped and eaten, and have never tried to understand. And that absurd hair that grows like scrub, gorse bushes, heather, all over, around, and down the back of the head. It's mine and *I want it.* To be joined instantly to that smooth body is more important than France, England, mysticism, self-respect, the future. It is imperative, and I can't stand here fighting it a minute longer. Oh I had no idea I was so in love with him! I demand that body with its nervous power, its smell, its intensity. And it *must* be given to me. If not, I'll ... I'll ...

In two minutes it was all over; I recovered. It was the last struggle. I thought: "Thank God, *that's* finished." And walked away.

As I walked I ground up all these longings into small pieces and sent them around my veins, so that they were part of me, but in such small doses that I could live with them. In that way they no longer constituted an enemy that had to be fought and resisted.

I remembered Pussy saying that there was a mental growing point between two people, and when one of them outgrew it, then the thing was finished ... however much you bluffed, and pushed, and lied, and retreated, and played, and desired.

Unfortunately the piece of life ahead of me suddenly went dead. I walked quickly to my room, and drew up a rigid time-table. I had taken the passive cure: now for the active one.

That day there was a letter from my mother telling me that her sister had died suddenly and had left me some money, about twelve thousand pounds. I hardly knew my aunt Jill, but my mother was very close to her and very upset. I wrote back at once trying to comfort her, and asked her not to mention the gift of money to Philip, or in fact to anyone. I had never had any money before, and it was a new experience. We had friends who were rich, but that doesn't actually make any difference to your own income. I knew that Princess Melika wasn't at all well off, but she lived with such authority that she was able to keep up a way of life that my mother could have afforded, but wouldn't initiate or sustain. Pussy would ring up Paris to know if someone's cold was better, and my mother would buy some wonder fertilizer for her garden. Pussy wrote that she had been sitting up in bed having Kate powder her alabaster back, while in her miniature pink television set beside the bed astronauts had been landing on the moon. And that one of them looked like Ziz (Colonel Carter) and would certainly make some astounding discoveries there. The terrain was exactly like certain parts of Tibet. She said that all astronauts were in a very advanced stage of development. My mother wrote that Rudi had waylaid her in the road while she was still dressed in black from the funeral, had got her into his house and said: "You look marvellous with your eyes like that," and tried to kiss her. She was so horrified she had gone down with laryngitis and lost her voice.

And then there was Guy's postcard scribbles. Apparently Rudi had suddenly announced that he was old, and had internal pains which could be mortal. He asked Guy to take him to the lectures on the plea that they might give him "peace of mind." This put Guy into the most hideous moral dilemma. He was afraid the lectures would teach Rudi to develop even more power in his person, to be able to gain over others even more easily than he could now, and that he would turn all this to *bad* use. He said his father was morally irresponsible. He said it was as dangerous as giving a tiger the clear brain and wings of an archangel.

Guy's postcards made me laugh. They were written headlong down the space provided in the jagged forlorn characters of a schoolboy who is homesick and does the thing in a hurry and in secret. He exaggerated his father's character. The lectures were Guy's carnal joy, and he guarded them like a mistress. It was as though Rudi had asked to go to bed with that mistress, to degrade her, to "see what she was like." Guy said that under the pretext that he was an old man seeking peace of mind he was simply after more cake. And hadn't a moral bone in his body.

I wrote back suggesting he took Pussy to the lectures and let her decide whether Rudi was fit for them.

A week later I got back from the village one afternoon, and François came running at me with some delicate gibberish. François had a stutter, and he would stand still and speak to you with eyes that assisted the broken French narrative by radiantly beaming on you and were overswept by washes of his black eyelashes, with last night's dreams still fixed in them. His act was an enchantment. I dug a few words out of the tinkling.

It turned out that a telegram for me had come over the telephone and Henri de Salignac had written it down on something and put it on the high marble mantelshelf in the dining-room, out of reach of the children. I went to look.

There was nothing much up there beside the clock but a lead soldier and a child's playing card. The two of clubs, actually. This bit of pasteboard, two inches long, had something written on it. "If can put up arrive Friday late all my love Philippe."

Philip!

Today *was* Friday. Which Friday did he mean?

I did not want Philip here. It would be ruinous. I actually *didn't want to see him*. I walked to and fro with the playing card, wondering what I could do to prevent the visit. I must phone him at once, at the Treasury.

I went to look for Iris upstairs. She was delighted at the thought of another visitor. They had so many rooms. It was so easy. I asked: could I telephone? Yes, yes, use the telephone in the little blue salon, but take a rug with me for my feet! They kept you waiting.

For the first time I *ran* downstairs. Never mind the rug. The children caught the turmoil, and fled before me. Philip's number was ... I had slight difficulty in remembering it. That number which had been burnt into my mind with a red-hot poker for two years!

I sat by the telephone, unhooked the decrepit receiver, and began one of those series of bit-part, disconnected conversations with sirens inside the wires ... who went away and left me in the middle of a sentence ... who lost their tempers and screeched ... who talked to close friends, and totally ignored me ... who suddenly became intimate, warm and friendly, prying into my private affairs ... who played music to me by accident ... who told me sharply that they would ring back, and cut me off.

By that time I had a throng of children around my knee gazing up at me, filled with awe. Afternoon shadows from the trees were shooting across the ground outside the window. As I sat there they seemed to grow inch by inch as the clock ticked. François asked, as though the whole thing was a *fait accompli*: "*Est-il un grand seigneur?*" They were waiting for this man of mine, in wonder, and they would judge me by him. He would come out of the blue, as the postman came, but wearing the finest hacking jacket, carrying a gun like Henri, handsome as a god and followed by another Aiöu shining like a *louis d'or*. The thought of it put them into the seventh heaven.

In the early evening, when all the offices were closed in London, there was a feeble chirrup from the telephone.

One of the sirens was there; she had rung the number repeatedly but she could not get any reply. And she was ringing back to know whether I still wanted a personal call. No; I did not. The mist was approaching. The children were wearily climbing the stairs. Rhythmic thunderings, clashes of music came from the direction of the kitchens. The stone floors seemed to be one degree colder than ever before. The Norman doors had already been locked and barred from inside when the shade of the tower in the west wing filled the main entrance with the dark breath of the Underworld. The day had ended earlier than usual.

Iris sent Christine up to prepare a room, just in case.

Dinner was eaten in a mood of expectation. Each of us listened for the scrunch of feet on the pebbles outside. Beyond was the flat, the silence of Normandy in dead winter. No one came.

When it was time to go to bed, Henri said that as he slept so badly, lying there as lightly as a leaf, half-awake, he would go down and let Philip in if he arrived after dark. He would certainly hear him, with his insomnia the way it was. On these moonlit nights he was as wide awake as if it was midday. Iris always said that he slept deeply, but he denied it. He assured me that he heard *every sound* and he would undoubtedly hear "*le fiancé de Sophie*" arriving by moonlight. This was Philip's new title. There were some country jokes after this. Iris asked me if my heart was beating faster. We all went to bed.

I closed my door uneasily. My secret, timeless holiday had been punctured by that telephone message. I almost wished I had dragged the instrument out by the roots and thrown it on the rubbish heap with the turnips round at the back. That was where it belonged. It was so feeble, it hardly worked at all. It was just about able to spit a few lethal words onto a playing card behind my back, and then it was finished, spent, and gave up the ghost. It was one of those one-way telephones, built of wood and fuse wire, only half alive, uttering spasmodic croaks like a fledgling hurt by a cat. The act of sending a message back along the wires in an opposite direction had been too much for it. The telegraph poles we had listened to might thrum or tingle, but it was obvious that for any major piece of communication they were useless. They were toys driven into the body of the countryside; just pegs to earth the surplus electricity in the winter sky.

I must have fallen asleep at about midnight.

I woke again later in the night, and lay there thoughtfully.

There was a mouse scratching somewhere in the passage. I could hear it quite plainly: scratch, scratch, scratch. That was the first mouse I had heard at St Emilion, and I listened with interest.

Then it came to me that it wasn't so very much like a mouse scratching ... that it was coming from further away, much further ... and could be someone down at the front door ...

Philip!

I jumped out of bed. In a sudden flurry of long white nightdress and red dressing-gown, I put myself together. Slippers ... where were they? Ah, gone to earth under the silly oak surround. I opened the door of my room. The passage was hung with sheets and sheets of moonbeams, fixed there by five degrees of frost. It looked endless.

Oh I could hear it now. Bang, bang, bang. Someone was beating on the doors. I hurried along the passage like a wraith. My heart, woken up from its great sleep of one month, began to throb in terrific beats to which it was wholly unaccustomed.

Where was the switch for the light over the stairs? I had

never left my room after dark before: had more sense. I groped about for the stupid little thing. My fingers went along dusty moulding, while the noise at the front door was loud enough, from here, to wake a barracks full of soldiers. I still couldn't find the light, and decided to go down, clinging to the rail, and turn it on at the bottom.

Slippers are not made for ancient wooden stairs with treads which slope out from the radius and try to shed you into a black cavern. I wanted to call out in order to stop the banging, but I doubted if my voice could be heard outside.

At the bottom, I went straight to the vibrating doors and began to lift the iron bar. The banging stopped; whoever it was was listening. I got the bar up and back. There was an enormous key sticking out of the lock; I turned it. The door remained fixed. I looked for a bolt, and finding an iron pole with a knob just above my head, I pulled it down slowly and heard it travel out of the socket and grate itself as it left its bed.

I pushed one half of the door outward.

There was a gush of icy air. And there was Philip, so familiar, smiling at me, his coat collar up, and laying against me his cold cheek and even colder ears.

"I've been here for *hours*, hammering with my fist."

"I thought it was a mouse!"

"I nearly gave up in despair."

"I just heard a tiny scratching sound in the distance."

"I even went back to the car once and sat in it. I thought I should have to spend the night there."

"I was just going to turn over and go back to sleep!"

"There's a hard frost out here. Let me come in; quick."

I put my head out for an instant. The wooden door was sparkling as though someone had shaken white sugar over it. The whole château was a glittering, frosted-up fortress.

"God! You're right. You might have frozen to death!"

"Ha-ha."

"You're very gay."

"Of course I'm gay. I haven't seen you for a month."

He had unbuttoned his coat and tried to put me inside it. I said:

"No. Let me do the doors. It's my responsibility. How did you get here?"

"I got a Hertz car in Paris and drove down."

"You should have let me know you were coming."

"Didn't you get my telegram?"

"Yes. But too late to—didn't know which Friday you meant."

"I thought I'd come straight away. I've never seen that night-gown before. It's very sexy."

"No it isn't. It's my provincial French night-gown."

"Those are the sexiest sort."

"No they're not. Stop being so friendly at this hour of night. You're supposed to be dead tired. What's got into you?"

"Just happy."

"Oh Philip. Please don't say things like that." I fell back crushed on his behalf by what was in my mind. "Anyway, we'll wake the house."

"What, after all the noise I've been making!"

"Your room's upstairs."

"Oh good. Come on."

Large cold hands were holding me through my night-clothes, and I was beginning to shiver. I guided Philip up the stairs. He said "my God" once or twice, because they really were like one of those rickety ladders hung across an abyss one sees people trying to get over in films. I had remembered where his room was. When we got there after a good deal of stumbling about, Philip at once began to take me into his arms.

"No, honestly, I must go. Suppose Henri appears? Things are very formal here, you know. It would be all round the village in the morning. Look: Christine's turned your bed down. And you've got that lovely old chest of drawers, it's fifteenth-century, and was made for church vestments."

"Are you glad to see me?"

"Of course I am. Will you be all right here?"

"If you stay."

"I can't *possibly*. It's so dangerous. I'll see you in the morning. We pushed that commode back to give you plenty of room. It's Louis Quinze, and the legs are different lengths so don't kick out those wedges underneath."

"You sound like my father."

"I am rather like him. I've been finding out."

"I hope not. Why are we whispering?"

"Because we don't want to wake anyone. Even the maids. They sleep in, you know. Look: there's the light-switch next door to the bed, and I showed you where the lavatory was on the way up."

"Where's your room?"

"Oh it's miles away ... right next door to the children."

"I'll be lonely here on my own."

"Philip! A big strong man who's just driven down from Paris in a Hertz car!"

"It's so cold."

"You'll soon get used to it."

"Do you love me?"

A short, dangerous pause. But I did love him.

"Yes of course. But I must go."

"Oh well, all right." He turned his head away, hurt.

I stood there, waiting, shivering. With his face still turned to the side, he said rather sharply:

"Go on, then."

Pussy was right; this child was my responsibility. He was cold, overtired, and only vaguely disappointed; after all, the right words had been said to him. But I hadn't fluttered. I hadn't made quite the right gestures. I hadn't said anything light-headed and feminine and totally irrelevant, so that he could assert himself with a: "Now, come along, Sophie. I can see we'll have to put you to bed." I was more like a smiling, polite boy.

I went up and kissed the cheek that was sulking.

"Good night. Sleep well. I'll see you in the morning." I had to bite the word "darling" off the end of the sentence.

He wouldn't respond, and began chewing his lips. The only thing to do was to call him to order, and then leave at once. I said:

"Now, look. It's two o'clock in the morning. You need your sleep. I'll come in and wake you first thing in the morning."

I kissed him again, and left the room quickly, without looking back. I knew he would go on standing in that reproachful attitude until he heard the door close. And then he would put himself to bed as quietly and efficiently as if there was nothing else on his mind at all. It was as though we were playing that dance called "statues"; while the music runs on the children dance about alive, they freeze when it stops, and move again directly it starts up.

As I went back to my own room, I felt I had got over the first hurdle. I had established a barrier. It was easier than I thought it would be in these strange surroundings, which had no memories for us and where he was not making the conditions. And in addition, he *was* strange to me. It was Philip, my dearly loved Philip, but it was also a stranger; it was almost as much a shock as if the postman had embraced me. I'd forgotten anyone had the right to do so.

10

My polite boyhood began again in the morning.

From the very beginning Philip's visit was a success. I found him with the children and Aiöu around his bed, unshaven, being admired and questioned. The car he had arrived in was thought to be not grand enough, but he managed to hint that it was only his second or third car.

He had eaten the brown egg and the brown toast brought by Christine without ceremony, and was busy studying an acid-green map of the area. The children were examining those parts which hung free over the edge of the bed, and murmuring over the exotic canvas backing. It was, without question, the map of a *grand seigneur*. There was a solemn turtle-dove utterance which formed a background to our conversation; this *chaperonnage* was very welcome to me.

Philip's French was frightful. The curious thing about it was that the frightfulness was catching. I had been talking to Henri and Iris reasonably badly for a month, but Philip infected me and I began to slow down and conjugate verbs; everything became conditional. Where was the fluid, slipshod present tense we had been living in?

Henri appeared, refreshed after a night of insomnia. He gave Philip a flowing cloak and gumboots with liquorice shapes on the soles. We all went outside, and these two handsome men strode about together, inspecting the premises.

There was a weak blue fire in the sky. The grey stakes of the fences ate ice from the wind.

Philip looked into drains, and frowned. He stepped back to get an overall picture of the crumbling west wing—the wing that was always making shadows. He shook his head over the tower. The lodge-keeper came up, and was told to unlock the doors to the cellars. We all went down. Philip borrowed a stick from Henri in order to poke iron grids and walls that had fallen in. He was thinking, perhaps, that it was a liability; that you could not raise a mortgage on it.

I was lumped with the children. I realised that in one month I'd become a good-looking inarticulate bore. I was satisfied with my own boringness; it was so strong. Being happy is a form of genius. Every time Philip looked at me an amorous dark night of the soul showed in his eyes. I could do nothing wrong.

Iris nodded to me, laughing, to congratulate me. *Le fiancé de Sophie* had passed the daylight test.

This sort of behaviour went on for most of the day. Philip, the perfect Englishman with the Czech father, walked around his estate with a Scottish Norman, talking in schoolboy French about threshing machines. We had to get everything right: no slacking. I couldn't help noticing that Henri's French was deteriorating.

The children were organised to run and jump for things. They brought out their improving books. I thought Aiöu was going to revolt when Philip threw a ball for him, but he just gave him a thoughtful look and ran after it at a moderate speed. I noticed Philip only did it once. There is nothing more ego-destroying than throwing a ball for a dog which remains calmly by your side, wondering what on earth you are doing.

The only bad moments were when they tried to leave

us alone together. Then I would get up in a frenzy and manufacture things to do. I sewed up my cardigan; I had to make a paper house, promised Yolaine for her birthday; I had to go out and look for the eggs because Suzannah, the oldest servant, who did this task, was ill, and the hens laid all over the place—you had to know just where to look ... in French places.

He watched me quietly. His eye was on me; he had put me at the centre of his life. I mourned for him. But I had moved out of his power, and belonged to myself. I was safe so long as the physical barrier remained.

In the evening, clean, *dead tired*, and changed for dinner, I came downstairs and we were for a moment alone together in the great hall among the shadows.

As though we had talked of nothing else all day, Philip said peremptorily in a low voice:

"You have complete power over me."

Unfortunately he meant sexual power. I answered just as fast, before he'd even stopped speaking:

"What nonsense."

He took a step towards me, looking at me intently as though judging the reactions of a virgin, a creature of unknown temperamental difficulties. He wanted to hold me there with his eyes. At the same time—I think it was by just dragging in his lower lip as though he might bite it, as though his sexual hunger was too much for him—he made an explicit reference to the past. He did not move. His instinct told him that I had become somebody; and if he attempted to caress that unfamiliar person with a familiar gesture, everything would be at an end between us.

We remained looking at one another, as though nailing ourselves together, unable to move.

In those steady emotional eyes, full of love, were offered

to me all the thoughts he had been so unwilling to share with me before. He was offering his body, a quickly moving, hot-tempered, and luxurious body, as he stood there, and he was offering the whole of his inner life. There was the dent in his bluish chin that I knew so very well; I had bitten its elegant bumpy surface so many times. His hair was very definitely too long for St Emilion, and belonged, still, to the London cocktail party for which it had been grown ... I think it was this that saved me, that reminded me ... of my terrible danger ...

And what did my face tell him as we stood there? That I was afraid of him. I was afraid to put myself back into his power. And that I no longer trusted him with that trust that made us a man and a woman together. I hadn't trusted him since the "I can't promise you" speech. The power lay with me at this instant. One submissive gesture, one joyful glance which promised him I would make love to him in a certain way and which gave him a foretaste of the lust, worship, and concentration of my touch on his body ... one of *those*, and I would hand myself over to him forever. The power would pass to him and from that moment I would live in dread. Yes, if I took this perfect man I would be lost; lost *psychologically*. I would die, and become his dog. And I would wake up—when? In ten years, at the age of forty-one, in exactly the same place, middle-aged, anxious, wholly dependent on him?

I knew he had come to ask me to marry him.

And I knew, since he was such a logical man, that he must have heard about the legacy from my mother's sister.

His eyes were now looking me up and down quite coarsely and bad-temperedly and seemed to get an angry pleasure from what they saw. It was, unfortunately, not at all offensive. Although it was done deliberately to tell me that this part of me, and that part of me, were highly desirable, like groceries which would fetch a good price in his estimate as a grocer. It was like feeling the harsh midday sun on you after a long abstinence, and responding with a muscular pride in your body which begins, involuntarily, to offer itself to that sun, and which prepares to surrender itself by first growing tense and expectant.

Sensing that he had suddenly begun to succeed, he quickly looked up at my face with a sensual enquiry, and found there enough to make him bow his head again in a dogged, woebegone fashion which was half-true and half put-on. He said in a low voice that faded away:

"I can't go on without you."

"Now, Philip . . ."

"It's true."

A lock of hair fell forward, as it always did when he bent over his papers, or over me. He dashed it back without vanity. And said desperately:

"Why are you avoiding me?"

"I'm not."

"Well, what do you think you've been doing today? I didn't come all this way for a tour of the estate, you know."

"Don't be rude." How sharp my voice was.

More silence. He held his head in its suffering attitude: muttered words reached me from it.

"You don't know how much I've been looking forward to seeing you. And now . . . you won't even let me touch you. You're slipping away from me."

"Oh Philip."

"What has *happened*, Sophie?" He was convinced that some event involving people and time was the explanation. An immovable frame of mind can't be seen, therefore it's not dangerous, and does not count as an event. When he was upset, there seemed to be a band of pain across his eyes where one might put a blindfold. This area had a curious shocked appearance—as though glycerine had been thrown there, or as though a pane of ice had been smashed there.

"Nothing."

I said it with the same desperate self-pity that he had used to me: the result of lonely nights and tightly wound nerves. He was moved, and suddenly with a loving, pitying gesture, opened his arms to me.

"Darling . . ."

"Please don't touch me."

"Oh God. You don't know how that cuts."

He lost his self-possession, and turned his whole body away violently. But instead of leaving the room, as he would certainly have done in the past, he remained there before me. I was shocked. He wanted me to see him out of control, and very nearly in tears. He no longer hid anything from me. His face was a dark turkey-red and water was in his lashes and his nostrils. He knew well enough that in such a dejected condition I could never leave him, and that I would run to him, and engulf him in my arms, and kiss him, and talk that complete range of nonsense which is so feeding and which makes a man young and selfish enough to go on living: "My little one, my gentle tiger, my beauty, my lovely young one, my only love, my poor little baby, my tiny creature."

He was saying to me: "See what you have done! Now mend me."

I went to him. But at that moment Iris appeared at the top of the stairs and gave a merry peal of laughter. She had caught us together; at last! We must all go and drink to it in the little blue salon.

She came down, and I saw that she had changed for dinner, was in black from chin to toe, smart, pretty and aristocratic. I saw that her black hair had hints of water and fireworks in it like a starling's body.

Philip underwent a metamorphosis. Now that he thought the essential business all but settled, he could take up his normal behaviour. Smiling secretively, as though the sight of her gave him a pleasure he couldn't quite control, he flirted with both of us simultaneously. To me his eyes said: "She might be quite something in London. It might be worth it, socially." He was already eating hidden pleasures and a light had gone on in the top of his head where he kept this secret food. There was something bashful and mealy about him when he went about this task. He was hiding inside his head, hoping no one would notice what was going on.

As for me, I was on the point of going up to Iris, taking her hand and kissing it, I was so grateful to her. As she came downstairs my body was de-narcotised on the instant.

For hadn't I realised, as she descended, tread by tread, that here was the equivalent of the rich, well-brought-up young woman in the grey mackintosh whom Philip was destined to worship? Of course. It was *she*. No matter that this one was married and had five children. There would be others. Iris was simply proving that they existed; the supply hadn't run out. European soil could be relied on to breed more of them.

Philip spent the rest of the evening attending to her wants. By the time dinner was over he had a woman friend who would well outlast his life. He was as busy as a bee.

I had time to think. I knew perfectly well he would come to my room as soon as the evening wound up. I had to give him a reason why my door would be locked. The only solution was to be ill. And the only illness that can excuse a locked door and a feeble voice calling out from inside is a bad stomach. The sooner I started it the better; one could go off to bed, groaning in agony, and fall asleep early. After that a light amorous tap-tap-tap was hardly courteous. Besides there was Iris to think of now.

The irritating thing about a tour of property is that it makes you unnaturally hungry. I decided that my illness would strike directly after the cheese. Tonight there were six courses: it was certainly no time for an illness. Pastry that shone as though varnished like wax fruit, and arranged in a sort of cable stitch, appeared holding minced beef, and then jellied damsons, in addition to a savoury cheese emulsion with onion in it. There was a mound of white butter the size of an elephant's foot on the table. It was all excellent. I couldn't bring myself to get up and leave it, but sat there eating and plotting like Judas, while knives and forks worked away. And Aiöu brought up his flopping jaws and polished around the marble, snapping when he came on a solid.

The day of fresh air, the absence of hard topics of conversation, the appreciation that newly discovered human beings have for one another, made it a last supper to be remembered.

At the end of it, drowsy and absolutely full up, I pushed my chair back and said that I felt terrible and that I must go away at once and be alone. I said it was probably a chill, caught at the front door at two o'clock that morning.

Philip rose to his feet, slightly annoyed. He was never ill himself, and he was always disconcerted by it. It seemed such a pity, when things were going so well. But he asked tenderly:

"Shall I come up with you?"

"No, thank you. Please don't bother. I'll take some Kaolin powder and some Codeine and in ten minutes I'll be asleep. Be perfectly all right in the morning." I knew he could never bear to miss anything.

I left them murmuring kindly to me, and I passed through that familiar obstacle course to my room.

An hour later, I heard Henri and Iris go by my door. The three of them had wanted to stay together as long as possible downstairs, drinking Calvados. Like healthy athletes they enjoyed the sight of one another's round cheeks and graceful, assured gestures. Books, plays, operas, films, paintings, all the wretched indoor life of cities, were what one's servants did to amuse themselves. The real life was *here*. With a mind swept clean, antiseptic and empty, one recovered the great sensual dignity of an animal that knows how to idle.

I was at that moment, avidly reading *The Zen Teaching of Huang-Po* like one of those servants, with only a finger and thumb exposed, holding it on my pillow. Quickly! Lights out! I stretched out my hand and cut it off and lay there with my book in the darkness, eyes still open and goggling. Ah, ah. Only just in time. I heard some footsteps. Up they came, then there was the debate, and my name called softly: "Sophie."

I lay there triumphantly, eating horrid darkness, locked to my book of magic. I felt like Aiöu refusing to run after the ball. I am not your sexual doggy-woggy.

* * *

Philip had spent two barren moonlit nights at St Emilion. The weekend was nearly over.

On Sunday morning I kept well away from his dangerous room.

Iris and Henri went to Mass. I, in training for mysticism, completed the physical exercises we had been given while listening to the church bell ringing over the countryside. The psychological exercises had already reduced my guilt and fear (especially fear of the future) to a level that was inconvenient for Philip. With every hour that passed I was setting myself free. I then walked over to the village, kicking tufts of frosty grass with my boots. I began to laugh about Iris asking after *le prince Charles*, and Philip's comprehensive look of disapproval. If he had put a Wellington boot in front of his face he couldn't have done better.

When he found me later in the morning, I was playing cards with the children downstairs, and was therefore physically invulnerable.

I smiled up at him ... and then the devil of it was, I laughed slightly. It came out as a voluptuous little gurgle. And a crimson rash appeared on his cheek, starting at his chin and going up in a triangle.

I hadn't meant to do it; it was insufferable of me. But the sound got out of my cheek so naturally, before I could stifle it, and, what was worse, it was instantly picked up by the children! They all laughed up at him in harmony, until it must have seemed that all the world was mocking him.

He gave me a cold, flashing glance and lost his temper.

"I suppose you think it's funny."

"Think what's funny?" I was much too gay.

"You know perfectly well what I mean."

"Don't be such a *lump*." I had never dared to say such a thing to him before, and was nearly scared out of my wits when I said it. To Philip—who took himself so seriously! Philip, who had just made everyone on the estate adjust their lives so that they ran with greater efficiency—and had done this to please *him*. I said:

"You've got no sense of humour. It's terribly funny. And

you've actually enjoyed yourself very much, and you won't admit it. You're going to stand there and pretend you're hardly done by!"

More angelic chuckling from the children, who knew perfectly well what was going on.

"Now do come and join us, darling," I said carelessly. "This sort of give and take with the children is exactly what you need."

He lifted his head hopefully.

"That's the first time you've said 'darling' to me since I arrived."

"Nonsense. You weren't listening."

"I've never listened so hard in my life." He added irritably: "And I do *not* need give and take with the children."

"Well, you sound as though you do. You're snappy."

He was carrying his acid-green map, and began to unfold it with a dogged carefulness. As he did so, he said in a very low humble voice:

"Don't make fun of me. I love you."

I was hit. I had walked into a wall. It was the child I had so often held in my arms who spoke to me and called out for help. He knew I still loved him. And he longed for that love and couldn't understand why it wasn't to go on forever. I was terribly moved, and had nothing to say. The children looked at me to see what I would do next; they were afraid our side was losing. They were shamefaced for me, and lowered their eyelids. Wasn't I going to fight?

Philip crackled his map importantly and made notes in a pocket-book. Meanwhile we played the cards as softly as we could; already it was established that we must not disturb him with his map and his low-voiced sentences. And that what he was doing was on a high level, and what we were doing was of no account.

The cards had French gnomes and horseshoes on them.

There were yelps of dismay or glee, and darting movements. And the pitter-patter they made as the children threw them down. I managed to pull myself through that sixty seconds of weakness, and catching sight of Philip in profile—he was trying to hold this beneficial mood for as long as he could—I had a second illuminated spyhole into his character. It was as strong as the moment when Iris came downstairs in black last night, and helped me to see through him.

This time, as though to complete my reading of him, I could see right round this episode and out at the other side. He had come here absolutely determined on a certain course of action. And *nothing* was going to stop him. If it was necessary to be touching, even humble, then that was what he would be. If it was necessary to shed tears, then he would shed them. He would do whatever was expedient to get his own way. And he was instinctive enough to change his violin for a 'cello, his 'cello for a bassoon, his bassoon for a trumpet, until his orchestrations had broken me down emotionally.

That could all be forgotten in twenty-four hours once we were united, and he would instantly take up his impressive manner, his Treasury uniform—the manner with which he had held me off for over two years. And he would continue on his way uninterrupted for the rest of his life without another tear dropping from his eye. I was holding things up.

He said in the same low, unhappy voice:

"Will you drive up to Paris with me this afternoon?"

I took a breath.

"It would mean staying overnight ..."

"Well—why not go the whole hog? Fly back to London with me?" He said it as though it was the most natural thing in the world, as though there was an agreed relationship between us. The simplicity was meant to disarm me. It did nothing of the sort.

When I answered him perfectly calmly, putting my own requirements before his, stating them clearly and not apologising for them, he could hardly believe his ears. I said:

"I hate flying, as you know. And I don't want to use myself up by dashing about and living it up. Especially when it means breaking into my holiday here."

He was absolutely furious and nearly shouted at me.

"Oh don't use yourself up for God's sake!"

The children looked at him in horror. The game stopped with all of us holding our cards and gaping at this ogre in our midst. Such a thing had never happened on a Sunday morning *in their lives*. There were steps outside: that must be Iris and Henri. The game broke up abruptly with the children rushing off to their sane and gentle parents.

I said:

"They think you're a monster!"

"Well then it's your fault if they do." He was testy and cantankerous.

"Please control yourself."

"I *am* controlled. I've got to do something to make you talk to me. I'm like—an animal that's being punished for nothing—I don't know what I've done wrong. And I don't know what to do next."

"Please keep your voice down."

"*No*. It *is* down. I need you; I depend on you. And you won't talk to me, you won't be with me. You're destroying me."

"You destroyed me ... much more thoroughly."

"*I* did?" He moved back, as though a trap-door had appeared under his feet.

"Yes. In that beastly hotel."

"But I can't even remember ..." This time he even staggered slightly as though none of the ground he was standing on could be trusted, and it was I who was responsible.

"No. Exactly. That is the whole point."

"Sophie, you're *cruel*." His eyes were all iris, he was accusing me on yet another virile instrument ... something so beneath ground, so groaning ... a double bass in his chest which he had never used before. We were both shaken to hear it, for it seemed to contain real grief. And I couldn't bear Philip to feel real grief. He was, simply, unable to cope with it. Why, all he wanted was a wife and a background; an ordinary life on ordinary terms. Romantic suffering would break him into a thousand pieces. I was the sort who could go into that sea and come out and dry myself off, and go on living—*just*. But Philip, never. I would have to give him reasons for disliking me: I must do something for his pride at once.

Voices were drifting in towards us from the room next door. He said rapidly:

"Come as far as Paris with me. You can get the train back this evening."

"All right. I'll come as far as Paris with you."

And so it was settled. Unwisely, I had agreed, out of pity and anxiety for him. And perhaps because I was afraid of the sort of explosive scene he might make there in the peace of St Emilion. I had to keep him quiet. If Iris and Henri hadn't come in at that moment ... but, who knows? I might have gone anyway.

New sides of both of us were coming out into the open. Philip was a scene-maker. I would do anything to avoid a scene. Philip knew what he wanted. I knew what I didn't want. Oh I was catching up with myself! I used to live my life long after it had happened, and get angry two days after the event. It had taken me a full two years, falling more deeply every week, to love Philip. Now I managed to find out, more or less, what I wanted and felt straight away. I knew that I wanted, above all, to be myself. And this was the reason why the lectures grew steadily more powerful. They taught you that it was your job to develop yourself, as the primary purpose of life; the chase is inward. This confirmed the natural tendency of my mind, which I had suppressed in the past, thinking that it was selfish. At the same time you avoided the company of those who limited you and themselves. I knew that Philip would stop me developing; and if that was so, wouldn't I hold *him* back?

One of the extraordinary changes between us was that he now generated the wilful emotion and I became the calm, cynical young man. He knew it, and it made him even more angry. And with his anger came even more womanish behaviour. I had made the emotional glue in the past, the solution inside which we loved and acted; he used to use it to put down my mind and raise up his own. He thought that when he arrived at St Emilion he could use it to show me that the only way to get straight was by marrying him.

My peace of mind was totally unforeseen; I was straight already. A disaster. He wanted now to muddle my brain and take away the cutting edge of my thoughts.

It was curious. Every now and then I began to live bits of what seemed to be my life ... and then someone would come and take it all away from me. Usually someone who said they loved me.

* * *

The moment we were in the car together and St Emilion was out of sight, he turned to me with one of those sweet-hearted glances I no longer knew how to receive.

"Don't smile at me like that!"

"Why not? That's how I feel."

"Don't smile at me like that, little creature!" My voice was full of anguish.

"Ah. You called me by my name." He sighed happily.

"But you hate being called that. Don't you remember you said it took away your dignity, and made a fool of you?"

"Did I? It doesn't sound like me."

"Oh but it was you. The real one: inside."

"Umph." A disbelieving noise, rather elephantine.

"You've forgotten all my irritating habits. Don't you remember you said to me: 'You're high-spirited. I like it. But for seven days a week ... I don't know if I could stand it'?"

There was a shade of the ill-humour we had left behind us when he answered:

"Sophie, I wish you would not invent things I have never said and quote them at me when it's convenient for you. A rational woman like you, too."

That was the old Philip! Especially the word "rational"; what a deadly word that was. Directly I heard it, life began to feel heavy again; all magic left by the first window, flew off and buried itself in an old drainpipe by the roadside in the last bit of blue poppy territory. In its place, suet, boredom, headaches, entered the car. Philip drove steadily, thriving on the atmosphere.

His spirits rose as he got closer to a city, and to his modern world, where he could control me in an environment he was accustomed to. I noticed there was something lavish about his mouth when he spoke. There was no time to stop on the way and so we went forward without a break.

Every signpost pointed towards buildings. We'd be there in no time, among clever, educated people who never laughed ... but made appointments, took wads of notes to and from the bank, parked and re-parked motor cars, arrested one another, played pianos for hours at a time, filled in forms, drilled one another's death, tapped on one another's chests, picked up telephones and at once started lying into them, lit up cigarettes, scoffed down magazines, dressed and undressed while looking into mirrors, hated one another without a break for ten years at a time, covered squares of canvas with coloured paints, haggled over pieces of furniture, ate pills from white boxes, fell in love with one another, and generally slithered about inside themselves, faster and faster, out of control. Bedsores, rissoles and mudflats!

We entered the suburbs of Paris just as evening was coming on. It was overcast. And rather like entering a bottle through the neck.

I looked about me, full of vague fears. Everything was shut, boarded up. Some shop fronts had iron grills fixed over them.

I couldn't help saying:

"What a muddy sky."

Philip frowned as he stared out of the car. He said, absently, his mind on something quite different:

"It keeps changing."

"What does?"

"We do," he said impatiently, as though I ought to have known.

"Do we? Well, it's probably quite a good thing."

This was a trivial answer, and he frowned even more deeply. He replied, in a battering, insistent fashion, spacing the words out with pauses:

"You can do with me what you like. And very well you know it."

I shivered, as though I was being bullied spiritually. It

was oppressive outside, and stuffy in the car. His company was enervating. I wished he would stop sawing away at his morbid violin. Why was he pretending to put himself wholly in my power? These incredible statements that were coming out of his mouth every half hour—they were so like the sort of things my mother said. I felt as though ropes were being fastened to my limbs, and leeches to my forehead. I looked at him discreetly without moving my head.

It was quite obvious that he was exalted by this entirely new frame of mind he had got himself into. As a noble lover, he drove strongly, rather fanatically. And I sensed danger and suddenly wanted to get away from him. Following my thoughts, I said without care:

"I'm not certain about the trains."

Philip was offended to the most sensitive, private recess of himself. He flushed up, swallowed, and answered:

"I thought you said you knew about the trains."

"No … you sounded as though you did. You said there was one this evening."

"I haven't the slightest idea about the trains this evening."

The door had been closed in my face. So be it. I had been behaving too naturally, and had been inconsiderate. Oh I longed to be able to relax! I would like to have taken him by the scruff and shaken him until he became human. The coldness between the two seats was like a sword.

After a moment or two I ventured to ask timidly:

"Where are we going?"

"To the Air Terminal. The Hertz people are picking up the car there."

"Oh." I didn't dare to say anything more.

In any case there was nothing to say. I hoped we would be able to look up the trains when we arrived. I only had the clothes I stood up in.

The sky seemed to be lower and darker at every moment. How empty the streets were. I read the names written on the awnings of closed, deserted cafés. *Café de la Paix. Au Bon Accueil. La Tour Eiffel.* The shops looked flashy, and were overcrowded with cheapjack clothes. In some of the windows there were large sheets of orange plastic covering the goods for sale. Down sidestreets I saw houses with windows dressed with narrow strips of grey gauze bandages. If we passed a roadsweeper he did not lift his head but went on pushing his broad broom along the gutter despondently.

It was a place where one needed, above all, money and papers of identification. I had very little money on me, about ten francs, and would have to borrow some from Philip. I asked:

"Could you lend me some money? For my ticket and so on."

"Yes." But it came out as an unhelpful tight-lipped hiss.

To my astonishment, and almost as though I wasn't there at all, he took a goose-quill tooth-pick out of his pocket and picked one of his teeth with it.

I withdrew into gloomy apprehensive silence. It was so dispiriting that after a little I was spurred to ask in a rather lonely, infantile way:

"Aren't you going to talk any more?"

He changed gear violently, and said:

"Not while I'm concentrating on driving."

I resigned myself, and waited for the fit of bad temper to pass. But it didn't pass.

Eventually, we drew up at the Air Terminal, the *Aéro-Gare*. By a coincidence, the Hertz car man was standing just outside the plate-glass doors and came straight up. This was the kind of modern efficiency that made Philip glow with pleasure. He was safely back among the machines and their servants. They signed the necessary papers, leaning on the roof of the car to do it. There was some affable conversation; both rejoiced in an appointment which had been kept nearly to the minute. Presently the car was driven away, and we were left standing on the pavement. It was nearly dark. A low gritty wind was blowing.

I had on my country mackintosh, and did up the buttons at the front. One or two smartly-dressed men and women passed us, pushed open the glass doors and disappeared inside the building. They brushed against me, and somehow made me feel that I didn't really exist. I had to catch my balance, like a country bumpkin who suffers from giddiness when for the first time in a crowd.

I was looking at Philip, waiting for him to suggest where we might go to find out about the trains. I didn't know his flight time, but I guessed he knew exactly how long he had. I didn't want to have to ask again for the money: I expected him to put his hand into his wallet at any minute.

He had lifted his case off the ground and put up his coat collar. He looked much taller suddenly and more commanding. For some reason he was staring over my head . . . as though he was trying to read the time on a clock somewhere in the distance but couldn't make it out in the gloom.

He made me wait for him while he did this. And I did so, in spite of my increasing agitation about the train. If we left it too late, I would have to spend the night in Paris; that would mean finding a hotel straight away.

In the end I felt I simply had to prompt him. It was absurd to stand there side by side on the pavement as though we had all the time in the world. Besides it was cold. A drop of rain fell on my face. I touched his sleeve and said in an anxious voice:

"Darling, do you think we could—"

There must have been something quavering in my voice, and something cringing about my shoulders which told him that I was no longer a tomboy, impregnable and happy, and that I was—for the moment—dependent on him.

He looked down at me with an unfriendly eye.

"Could what?"

"Why, find out about the trains of course!" I burst out.

He said abruptly:

"Now look here, Sophie. The obvious and sensible thing is for you to fly back to London with me."

I was almost speechless with surprise and horror. I jerked my head, and said helplessly:

"Oh no. I can't. Really. You know I hate flying. If it's too late for the train, then I'll find a hotel."

On hearing these words, he turned towards me. Without the slightest warning, he drew his lips back so that his lower teeth were exposed, like a furious chimpanzee, and in a paroxysm of rage he said, or rather spat:

"For your fucking refusal to fly you can damn well stay here!"

With that, he turned about, walked rapidly away, pushed through the glass doors, and disappeared from sight.

11

Why did I stand there, abject and paralysed by fear?

Oh there's no time to stand about when you're abandoned, alone, without money, after dark in a strange city you hardly know.

First I ran in the direction his figure had taken. I was going to beg him at least to lend me enough for a hotel. I ran; with my eyes starting out of my head in that effort to pick out an especial figure carrying a case and with the collar of the coat turned up. There were desks, lifts, moving stairs, inside the glass doors, and people hurrying about.

I ran to and fro with my heart thudding; a picture of white-faced panic and dejection. I questioned clerks at the desks. Everyone was busy. This one was having a telephone conversation; that one was carefully filling in a form for a man who stood impatiently nearby. They looked at me uncomprehendingly. I jabbered at them, and they waved me away, and sent me on somewhere else. I was so distressed I could hardly see. If I had seen him I would not have seen him.

I would like to have had his name called on the loudspeakers, but he might not respond. He was perfectly capable of sitting there, reading his newspaper and not batting an eyelid. Perhaps he had already left the building by another exit and was sitting in the airport bus. It might be driving away at this very minute.

People were beginning to turn their heads and stare at me. I wanted to sit down, so that I could mount guard there, over the lifts and stairs, but I could not fight off the curious glances. My old mackintosh and my flat shoes were not reassuring. In any case I had lost my nerve and could hardly make myself understood.

I decided—as much as I could pull myself together to decide anything—that I must return to the point at which he'd left me in the street. Perhaps he'd gone back there, pricked by his conscience, having taken all the revenge he needed to take ... and was searching for me even now.

I ran out into the street with my legs bending under me and looked about wildly. Only strangers were walking quickly in and out of the dark areas.

Once it was established, beyond all doubt, that I was alone, that he had gone and would not return, I tried to initiate a new kind of thinking. I was, by now, trembling so violently I was on the point of falling down.

I think it was the shock of being deserted, and cursed, by a man who had been protesting love to me for two days that rattled me out of all proportion. If I had come here alone, and had expected to be alone in such circumstances, then I could instantly have set about plotting for myself. But to be at one instant protected, and at the next left to sink or swim almost destitute, was the most horrible revenge he could have taken.

In the past I had always been terrified of getting into such a situation, and I had always guarded myself against it. I would never, never, never, have let this happen to myself. I was face to face with one of my archetypal fears.

In my extreme animal despair I remained near the lighted building, which at once became a form of home. By degrees I grew calmer as I reasoned with myself.

Why am I so frightened? These people in the streets are only human beings like myself. They're not going to set upon me and kill me. Unless they detect that I'm different from them and think it would be amusing to tease me. I must invent things to do which will explain to the casual passerby that I have a good reason for being here: that I am waiting for somebody, and that I am connected to this lighted building, which is a centre of power and activity. I shall look at my watch, put a pleasant expression on my face, and walk with firm steps to and fro with a slightly abstracted manner. While I am doing that I can collect my thoughts. I must at once stop exuding the stench of fear from my skin, which has changed to a substance like cold putty.

I began to do these things, and was greatly reassured.

The thing was to get myself a hotel, and from there to telephone Iris. But if I telephoned Iris I would have to confess that I had been deserted, ignominiously, by the man I had introduced into their household. Or I could telephone Pussy in England. How long would it take to get through, though? I dared not take a taxi anywhere in case it came to more than ten francs. Therefore I must walk about and find a hotel on foot. But how could I pay for the hotel the following morning? I would have to stay there until friends came and rescued me with the money. But would a decent hotel take me without luggage, and dressed as I was? I knew no one in Paris; it could have been Borneo, and felt like it.

Suppose I went to the police? No; one heard such stories about the capricious behaviour of the police. They would question me as if I were a guilty wayward young woman, a stray. I would have to sit for hours in some bare waiting-room, exhausted and without food.

What about the British Embassy? Closed surely, at this hour. Or just a clerk who would tell me that he couldn't help me, and that I must come back in the morning. And besides how did I get there? I hadn't the slightest idea where it was, and had no map. No, no. That was no place for *la fiancée de Philippe*, a government institution filled with smooth stone-hard faces just like Philip's when he was carrying out his duties.

How frightful to land up in a city where you know no one who can vouch for you, not a soul.

If I thought ten francs was enough for a call to London, I would have gone into the Air Terminal and phoned Pussy at once. But that was all I had in the wide world.

Then, at my wits' end, I thought of Guy. Poor Guy! The hunted hare running from the ghost of Baudelaire. If only he were here now I could ring him up and be with him in an instant.

But what about his room on the Île St Louis? That was still there. I knew it for a fact, because he'd left half his possessions behind. No matter if he had sub-let it to someone else, I could at least find friendly faces to talk to. I could use the telephone. And if necessary I would sit there and refuse to go away.

It was now quite clear to me what I must do. I must find my way to the Île St Louis, to the lodging house called the Duc de Luynes. If the worst came to the worst, I could at least return to the Air Terminal. That would be open all night.

One of the advantages of looking for an island in a darkened city is that one can always find the water by which that island is surrounded. This kind of primitive reckoning is familiar to all tourists, emigrés and stray cats and dogs. I had only to ask for the river, and once I had found the river I had only to confirm in which direction lay the Île St Louis. As it was, I thought it was upstream from where I stood, and the plan of the city became clearer and clearer in my mind as I thought about it. But you cannot afford to make mistakes on foot, and spend half the night walking the wrong way.

I had forgotten the Eiffel Tower. Of course; however lost you were, you could always take your bearings from the Eiffel Tower. There it was, over to the left.

With legs that had not entirely stopped shaking, I set out for the river.

I found it almost at once. I had been so close, really on top of it.

The Seine was flowing from right to left, glimmering and slow, through the middle of this hard-as-nails city. I knew exactly where the Île St Louis was; upstream.

I started walking. I soon developed a style of movement to protect myself from being accosted. As I went along I perfected it. The trick was to walk fast, with a bad-tempered but *knowing* expression on your face—as though you had already drunk some bitterness in this city and could therefore give as good as you got. You must not draw attention to yourself by bracing your shoulders or swinging your body, or in fact by giving any signs of good health and bravado. On the contrary, you must go by people in a slightly hunched attitude, just as they went by you. Above all, you must never look at anyone, or acknowledge by the flicker of an eyelid that they were there. Therefore I went on my way, hunched, abstracted, blinkered, to cover my deep fear. I walked tirelessly, faster than I have ever walked in my life.

Even after I had taken all these precautions, dark forms stepped out of the shadows and interrogated me, sticking out blue muzzles. Two men walking together would stop and bar my path, and try to take my arm. I shook them off, and walked on, studying my part more deeply, extracting from my face the last traces of individuality and intelligence so that there was nothing out of the way to be read there. Once your face is a piece of white rubbish they will leave you alone. How well I now understood Guy's odd, persecuted behaviour.

But at least the city was fractionally less hostile. I had dragged myself out of the first level of destitution. I could now rank myself with the itinerant student and his kerosene stove.

That awful walk! Every step was a nightmare. Especially the murderous effort to still the fear inside myself, so that these shadow-men, terrible dogs of civilisation, would not scent it, and close in.

In this condition I arrived at the Île de Cité, crossed the bridge to it, and went around the large square of Notre Dame. I knew the Île St Louis lay behind it. There it was!

There was a footbridge formed of heavy planks like railway sleepers. They moved against one another as you stepped on them. On either side was a high wire wall, rather like a tennis court enclosure. I hurried across. The sky began to rattle and groan. Midges and travelling spots of water landed on my face out in the open here. Someone was approaching from the other side. I could see the big noisy boots. As we passed one another he ejected a sharp grunt from his stomach: "Eh!" I had noticed that almost every man or woman sniffed or coughed or uttered some communicating noise as I passed them on that lost walk of mine … as though to ginger me up, in case my fear had died down, tired of itself, and had taken a few seconds off to rest and become complacent.

Huge trees grew on the island, and swished themselves as the noisy night sky went through them.

The Duc de Luynes; it was down the Rue St Louis,

I knew that. This turned out to be a long narrow main street, old, with narrow doorways and little shop fronts. The stonework of the pavement and gutters was worn like a cathedral's. I walked upon it and for the first time dared to raise my eyes from the ground. There were no names anywhere, but here and there were old-fashioned numerals painted on little white enamel plaques. I had no idea where it was. I would have to ask one of the terrible dogs of the streets. I was so far from any form of safety that I shrank to do so.

Ah; here was a woman coming along, quite young too. I hurried up to her, with my sorrowful face and midinette shoulders.

"Excuse me, Madame. But do you know the house called the *Duc de Luynes*?"

She gave a cheerful laugh. Certainly she knew it. It was just a few steps down the road. She would show me; she was an islander herself.

I understood then that I had had the luck to pick one of the chosen few, one of the sisterhood of a community living here who thought of themselves as islanders. The Pisceans of Paris. My stampede came to an end; my shadow at my heels stopped chasing me. I went with her trustfully. I was aware of the smell of water in my nostrils, very fragrant.

With her bold air and loud voice, she was exactly the companion I needed in that dark street.

"There!" She pointed at a narrow building. It was just a packet of stucco with a menials' entrance; evidently once built for servants. Whom did I want? She would ask Madame Monnu inside. She pushed open the door and we were in a dim hall with black walls.

At the back of the hall was a door which was half glass. And through this one could see into a further dimly lighted interior containing an old-fashioned black stove along one wall—the sort that used to be polished up with black lead—two or three elderly people sitting about, a bulldog and a young girl who was in the act of lifting an enormous kettle off the stove and was holding it with a patchwork kettle-holder. They all turned their heads towards us. The bulldog sprang at the glass, and the girl put down the kettle and seized him by the collar. This homely scene was like a vision of Paradise.

"You'll be all right now," said my friend from the street. She smiled at me and went off.

The young girl opened the door, holding back the bulldog, which panted, showing a pale pink tongue like a tulip petal with a fold down the middle. Directly I mentioned Guy's name, they all came to life. "I am his sister," I said, rather ashamed of myself, but much more afraid of being rejected. "And I have nowhere to stay for the night."

There was some anxiety, and a great deal of talk, but on the whole they accepted me without much fuss. Looking back, I am astounded that they did. I explained how it had come about that I had become separated from a friend, and had forgotten that I had no money.

The old people clicked their tongues, and crumpled up their faces of brown paper. My countrified skin and my drab, wholesome coat were in my favour this time. Madame Monnu said I could have Guy's room with pleasure, but the room of a young student was always in a terrible state ... and it was more or less as he had left it, as if a lion had gone through it! Not the place for a young lady.

I didn't care. I would have slept there on the floor beside the bulldog. Anything to get off those haunted streets with their "presences."

She took me up the circular staircase Guy had described

so well; it was like re-dreaming a favourite old dream, walking in a book where you know your way about. Half-way up she switched on a little torch she had brought with her. There were the yellow strips of light under the doors just as he had said there were. And the last spiral *was* cobbled—I slipped on it at once—and turned in such a tight corkscrew that you had to go sideways at one point.

She unlocked the topmost flimsy door, putting a huge key into the cardboard, and pushed it open. The room seemed to be papered together, it was like the fragile timbering of a cigar-box. Clothes lay where they had been thrown, books where they had been opened and put down. The bed was more or less made. There was a skylight overhead which appeared black in the electric light. Drops of rain hit the glass steadily, spit, spit, spit, spit.

"*Voilà!*" We both laughed. The silent Prisunic clock on the shelf above a blocked-in fireplace caught my eye. I went straight up and began to wind it in what I hoped was a sisterly fashion.

There was a low door in the corner of the room, and if you bent down—which we did—you found yourself in a triangular "room" under the sloping rafters, which was another of those notorious bathrooms. But all this one had in it was a cold-water wash-basin and a little kerosene stove of speckled enamel with a window with a red celluloid pane in the side.

Madame Monnu showed me how to light it, for which I was truly grateful. A circle of blue fire appeared inside; the stove squeaked as you turned it up stiffly and gave out strong alcoholic fumes.

By then she decided she'd done enough for me.

All this time I'd been wondering whether I could phone Pussy on the old people's backroom telephone. But I guessed an expensive call like that would frighten them and overstrain yet another rickety telephone. Even if I reversed the charges, they would never quite believe that they had been reversed. Suspicion and doubt would enter our relationship. The French know perfectly well that a telephone is not a toy; it's another bill to be paid. But perhaps Normandy would be possible? Now that I was almost myself again I could find reasons to give Iris. I wouldn't go at the phone like a maniac and pour out my bitter story. And I had enough money to pay for the Normandy call on the spot.

I felt that I ought to take out my purse, and open up the contents, as a feeble guarantee. I did so, looking shyly at Madame Monnu. Would she? I could pay at once. It would be a very great kindness. I was so sorry for the nuisance and interruption to their evening.

She would. She was magnanimous. And I thanked her as I have never thanked before in my life.

My horrible adventure seemed to be turning a corner. I had found kind faces and a dilapidated room. I had a roof and a line of communication.

After I had phoned Iris, I felt even better. Everything was suddenly easy; her voice from St Emilion calling me "*pauvre Sophie*" and laughing at me, made me laugh at myself. She would phone some friends; they would rescue me tomorrow morning, or tonight if it was urgent? No; tomorrow would be all right. I didn't feel able to face smart Parisians tonight. I had to get the smell of the streets out of my skin first. It was "historic" that I should be staying on the Île St Louis and very clever of me, because all her friends wanted to have an apartment there. Yes, the children were in bed, and missed me and my fiancé, Philippe, the *grand seigneur*. I felt nostalgic for Aiöu, for the stairs, for the lemonade-green cobwebs floating in the breeze.

The old people gave me more warm glances after this conversation. The bulldog knocked against my legs as though I was part of the furniture. I had a cup of coffee with them and then withdrew, not wanting to encroach any longer.

This time holding the sacred key in my hand, I climbed the stairs with a light heart. It occurred to me that I was hungry. I couldn't go out: but perhaps there were some tins in Guy's room?

When I had reached it, and closed the door, I stretched myself out on Guy's bed … hard, yes, but oh how comfortable! And what a pleasant tick-tock that clock had; a bold note similar to the note in the voice of the woman in the street. And the way those raindrops were spitting themselves at the glass made you feel so *safe* indoors … doubly safe because you were in the room of a dreamer, a serious man, separated from the foreignness of Paris by a great river, and reigning quietly high up at the top of a water-scented island.

I suppose it could be described as a squalid little room, but lying out dead-beat on that bed, with a rhythm of the tick-tock and the pattering rain in my ears, it seemed a deeply enchanted place. And the peaceful atmosphere impregnated my limbs and slowed my heart, until I, too, became an islander, a Piscean, sniffing the waters of the Seine and only feeling able to drop off into deep slumber now that I was back "on board."

Perhaps that was what kept the illustrious ghost walking hungrily on one of the bridges, night after night, for a hundred years? An islander with a green heart, he could not bear to leave the antique streets, where he had buried all his dreams, but went on walking in his favourite places, under the impression that he was still alive, peacefully inhaling the river ... with that magnificent sneer embedded in his cheek. *Le poisson dans l'eau.*

* * *

I packed up my belongings at St Emilion and returned to London a week later. There was no point in staying any longer. I kissed Iris and the children with deep love. I knew that I would never see them again that size and in that state of innocence. It was like seeing a Raphael for the last time.

As the taxi took me through London, I looked about at the unfamiliar English people. How foreign they appeared to me with their beards and sidewhiskers! And the women, exotic dark creatures with long noses and dressed in vivid colours. What modern buildings, what clean cars driven about in an orderly fashion! Evidently this was a rich, new, strong city. Every street had an oblong white enamel plate with its name printed on it. Prosperous-looking couples walked together leading small dogs got up in fitted coats.

When I opened the front door of my own flat and stepped inside, it had shrunk, of course. There were messages, flowers and a welcoming note from my mother—nothing, thank God, from Philip. I think I would have been ill if I'd seen his writing.

I phoned my mother. Yes, she was a little bit better after her bad "go" of laryngitis; everyone had had the same thing, and it had been one of the most virulent of all English winter infections, positively as bad as the mysterious Asian 'flu which "struck" on other occasions when one wasn't having laryngitis. Yes, she was still furious with Rudi for trying to kiss her "in a squashy way" on the lips, just because she sat down for a moment in his house when she was distressed. But fate moved in a mysterious way, and the poor man was now in hospital having his appendix out at the age of sixty-eight! So his kissing days were over.

"His appendix?"

"Yes, darling, his appendix. It's not prostate; I asked Sister. It really is his appendix. Apparently he's had a grumbling appendix for years, and if he had a sudden violent attack it might be the end of him."

"Poor thing."

"He says he began to have the same old pain down in his stomach. There's a place called McBurney's point—"

"Darling, you're making this up!"

"I am not!" She began to laugh weakly. "It's down there, midway—" she gasped—"midway between the navel and the haunch-bone!" She got it out at last.

"The *what* bone?"

"The haunch. *Haunch.* You know what an animal's haunch is?"

We were back inside one of our ancient conversations; with my mother's decisive voice saying ludicrous things in an irritable way, and promptly collapsing into laughter. Why was it that nothing ever changed between us?

"Oh well. I'd better go and see him."

"Do. Poor old thing. He'd love that."

When I arrived at the hospital in Hampstead, the "poor old thing" was propped up in bed comfortably in a double room, (the other bed was empty), looking as fit as a fiddle and playing a transistor radio into his ear. Fruit, chocolates, a game of chess and a pile of opened, annotated letters and invoices were loaded up on the trolley over the bed. You could only distantly hear the moaning and bumping of floor-polishers in the linoleum corridors.

"Sophie my dear! Come and kiss me."

"Now, Rudi. I've been hearing all about your kissing. And look what it's brought you to! A hospital bed."

I had dressed myself up to please him, and was all in closely-fitting black. I walked around the bed with that old fox-tail swinging at my neck.

"Yes, they have brought me to this. Those damnable women who ruined my life," said Rudi, eyeing me with the utmost pleasure. "When did you get back?"

"Only yesterday. So you see I came straight here after a wash and brush up. Is it 'out'?" He nodded. "How are you feeling?"

"Not bad at all. There are some very pretty nurses here. Come and sit close beside me, and tell me everything."

I took off my coat and fur and sat down in a tubular steel chair by the bedside. It was low, and brought my head to the level of the chess game. Rudi was wearing faded blue-striped flannel pyjamas and had slipped a pair of glasses into the top pocket as I arrived. Only where his wrists came out of the pyjama sleeve did there seem to be a weakness, a piece of delicacy, perhaps old age ... those wrists were so slender and must have had bird bones inside them. His hands were healthily speckled like one of his own pheasant.

The windows were steamy, fast closed; it was raining.

He was excited to have me so close beside him, while he lay "helpless" in bed. We began to talk intimately on the question of men and women ... Being in hospital had reminded him that he might indeed have to die one day, and he was inclined to tell me secrets about his life which he might have kept hidden, or, rather, he was so accustomed to thinking them over and over, he had got used to them and had forgotten he was supposed to conceal them ... He broke off a story suddenly to ask:

"And Philip?"

I was prepared, and made an English answer in a strong voice: "We don't hit it off, you know."

Rudi gave me a deep, mesmerised look, and promptly took it the wrong way.

"I knew it! I knew it! Just like his mother."

"Ah." I looked vague.

"You remember that sofa I had delivered to me about six weeks ago?"

"As if I could forget it! The urine-yellow one."

"Ugh! What a colour! And you know I don't like ugly things, they just make me feel ill. I never liked sitting on it, even when Muriel had it. It was like sitting on a great big sunflower; so public. It was like being on the beach at Broadstairs. I used to sit on the edge feeling *miserable*. It seemed to change the whole room. It even changed Muriel."

"Did it? In what way?"

"Well, I . . . I just . . . could not make love to her. Couldn't do a thing! It was incredible. And she would keep talking . . . in a rather hectoring way."

"And that put you off? Honestly, Rudi! Any little thing puts a man off."

He writhed in his hospital bed. We had begun to have lunatic snatches of conversation while really talking about something quite different.

"Absolute nonsense, my dear. She could talk until the cows came home on the old sofa, and I wouldn't care a damn!"

"Well, that's just insensitive!"

"I didn't mind whether she talked or didn't talk! I just had the impression she would seize on any excuse to waste time on that new sofa . . . she was always going out of the room to do her hair in the middle anyway."

"Oh Rudi. She needed reassurance."

"Muriel did *not* need reassurance. It was *I* who needed reassurance. My God, I was trembling like a leaf. And trying to acclimatise myself to the new surroundings ... I took her in my arms, and kissed her ... I closed my eyes to keep out the yellow light ... But—*nothing happened.*"

He lay back on the pillows and looked as bewildered as if it was going on right now. He talked on, more or less to himself, rather like a transistor.

"It was terrible. I couldn't do a thing. I was in a terrible state. I didn't dare to start making love to her. I talked about everything under the sun, politics, gardening, Jacobean furniture ... Do you know that in the end I was in such despair, my dear Sophie, that I actually had to say I was feeling ill? Yes, I told Muriel that I had a violent spasm, rather like colic, in my stomach. I asked her if she could mix me up a little bicarbonate of soda ..."

If he hadn't been re-living his past for me—flushing up and scrunching the sheets like used napkins-I would have said he was making it up as he went along. In a sense, he was. Because he had spent years editing it and re-telling it to himself in a way that wouldn't bore him, and by now he had got it just right.

"I remember I lay down on that accursed sofa really feeling quite faint, after all that emotion. I was simply worn out. You could have boiled me down," said Rudi, "and made mustard out of me. And soap out of my umbrella."

He looked at me for applause, laughing slightly.

"Yes, very funny, Rudi. All you needed to finish you off was a storm of pin-head flies stinging you with formic acid."

I had come into his story with a joke of my own, at which I was now laughing. That wasn't what he wanted at all. I was trying to cream off the best of the story my way. I was stealing from Grock while he lay ill in bed, too weak to pass round the hat.

He said severely:

"These things are very important to a man. A man's pride is all he has."

"Whereas a woman—"

"A woman is quite another thing," said Rudi, with an invalid's crossness. "Look at Muriel. Do you know what she did when she saw me in that condition?"

"I can guess."

"She *giggled*! That is typical of an Englishwoman. She kills everything by giggling. I can tell you I got up in the most terrible rage, pain or no pain. I could have strangled her. I told her she was the biggest bitch in Christendom."

"Rudi, you can't say that sort of thing ..."

"Too late!" He crowed softly from the pillow. "I said it years ago. 'What you want,' I said, 'is an Irish labourer, my dear. You want brute force, old girl,' I said, 'like a grizzly bear from America. You might just as well go and live in the Rocky Mountains.'"

He took a chocolate from the box and put it into his mouth *whole*. There was the sound of walls being crunched; the square corners pulled his cheeks out of shape once or twice. "Glug," said Rudi.

I said accusingly:

"And now she's dead, poor thing."

"Yes, she's dead, lucky thing. And I am still alive and suffering. All I have managed to do with my whole life is to exchange a nasty old wife for a nasty new wife."

He ruffled in among the frilled chocolate papers in the box. I asked about Muriel:

"Do you mean to tell me you never managed to make love to her successfully?"

"Yes, yes, on the old sofa." He waved me on impatiently. I was holding up the main traffic; all his sufferings and grudges.

"Oh, well, thank God for that ... You know Rudi, I'm

surprised you're prepared to take a dangerous thing like the yellow sofa into your house."

He thought it over quite seriously, with a deep interest in his own actions.

"Yes. So am I, my dear. I don't know why I did. I took it in for old times' sake, that ugly, hideous sofa that made me so unhappy. It just shows what a long-suffering man I am."

"You miserable Rudi! You did no such thing. You took it away from Pussy, because you were too jolly mean to let it go. And look what happens to you!"

He looked up, startled.

"Well? What?"

"Six weeks later you're in hospital and your appendix is out. The sofa has taken its revenge! Muriel has won! You cried 'McBurney' once too often, with your colic and your bicarbonate of soda."

He caught the joke and began to laugh feebly.

"I remember the moment I sat on it I started to get aches and pains again ... it was just like the old days. I had to reel over backwards before she'd leave me alone, you know. And once I simply buckled up like a concertina. Oh—don't make me laugh. My stitches—ow! That bloody bitch. She did it deliberately. She left me a dose of poison in her will. And now she wants to make me burst my stitches."

"Now calm down, or I'll call one of the nurses."

"Well, you shouldn't over-excite me like this."

He patted the bed beside him for me to sit there and kiss him goodbye. I gave him a peck on the forehead.

"*Dum spiro spero*," said Rudi mournfully, with the tiredness of an old patriach. "Send your mother to see me. Tell her I'm not at all well. A relapse."

"I shall say no such thing. Has Guy been?"

"Yes. He came once. It was extraordinary."

"And Philip?"

"Philip came too. For five minutes. I have nothing in common with Philip. I wish he would not come. He is too superior. He makes me nervous when I'm not well."

"How long did Guy stay?"

"Five minutes. They both stayed five minutes."

"They're your sons all right."

When I was ready dressed to leave, the corners of his mouth went down. He began to move his chessmen in a resolute, gloomy fashion. Just before I left he said what was on his mind abruptly:

"You know what that boy of mine has done? He has taken Pussy to meet this Jehovah's Witness. And he won't take *me*. And now the wretched fellow goes to Pussy once a week for tea, and they're as thick as thieves up there together." A piercing glance from the sickbed.

"What do they sit on?"

"Sophie, you can be a very spiteful young woman when you want to be. Go away."

"Now, Rudi, that's not fair."

"Well, why do you have to say a spiteful thing like that to a lonely old man? As it happens I wanted to have something of Muriel's in my house. Do I have to explain all my private feelings to you? Unless you can sometimes take me on trust, then our friendship is at an end, my dear."

I had been out-manoeuvred again by this peppery speech; our parents were too clever for us. The integrity had passed from me to Rudi in his striped pyjamas in bed, a lonely misunderstood old man. I suddenly realised that Muriel *was* the sofa.

At that awkward moment, the door opened, and a smiling nurse wheeled in a pretty young woman in a dressing-gown with long blond hair combed down to her shoulders. Rudi smiled broadly and jumped on to the next bit of his life.

"Aha. My girl friend! The most beautiful woman in this

hospital, with the exception of you, Sister. Thank you for coming to see me, Sophie dear. And don't forget to tell your mother. A relapse."

I was being dismissed! I left the room, amused and irritated. Why, just at that very moment I'd been prepared to take one of the marionettes seriously! He had only been using his "feelings" to get me to stay on a few more minutes, so that he wouldn't have to be alone between visitors. That intervention was evidently a piece of supernatural timing and humour.

As I walked home through the familiar streets, I realised how much I was looking forward to the lecture the following evening. I'd hated missing them. I was longing to see my mother too; but there would be pain there. Because I would ask her: "Why did you tell Philip about that silly money?" And she would turn her head away from me and stifle a terrible sob. She would be choked by my ingratitude and by her anxiety for me, her sweetness and her simplicity would make the sobs as hard as stones rising up in her throat. And I would heap more coals of fire on her head by saying things that weren't true. I would say: "But now you've separated us forever. Whereas before, he would gradually have become my lifelong friend."

I was concentratedly playing this scene over in my head as though it was inevitable, and leering malignantly at no one, when, with an effort of will, I stopped myself. I came to a halt in the street, genuinely ashamed. "You love these amateur dramatics as much as the marionettes do. You hypocrite. You dog. You'll end up exactly the same as they are, unless you stop it *now*!"

Oh, I saw it clearly enough. It was up to me to let the incident pass in silence. That was why it had happened to me, to test me psychologically. So that I could use it to become a better person. Not to rush back onto the stage at the first opportunity and dance about in a frenzy, sing my tuneless song and waste more emotion. And if I was able to control myself, and bridle my furious rage against her—*she*, who had done nothing but love me too much—she would be amazed. She must be waiting even now for the scene which I had just played over in my mind. And she would be astounded and overjoyed when it did not come! She would begin to think and wonder. And she would understand that something had happened to me, something good, which was the foretaste of a new relationship between us. We would love one another as equals from then on, and there would be a change of heart between us.

I wanted to cry at the thought of it. It was not too late, then, to change things. We must do it now, while we were still alive and could reach one another.

I wanted to walk round to her cottage straight away. But I was almost afraid. I was so happy. I loved her so much. Should I not leave it a day or two? Going to her in an emotional state was always dangerous. It would be more sensible to get her used to the idea that I did not mind about Philip. I would go tomorrow, or the day after, in the afternoon ... while she was ironing and off guard.

12

"Hullo!"

"Hullo!"

"Guy! It's marvellous to see you."

"And you too! It's your turn to be French now, Sophie."

"I am. I'm quicker. Less self-conscious. Have we got time to go by the Heath?"

"You mean for the snow?"

"Yes, of course."

Cars were going by with mufflers of snow on them. The roads had been cleared, and people had put gravel, and salt, and cinders down from their front gates to their front doors.

Only the Heath was still a fairyland.

We hurried down the road to it, like truants.

"How's Biddy, Guy?"

"Mother's incredible, as always. She does three things I loathe. a) She keeps talking to me. b) She holds on to me with her little tiny sprat's hands. And c) she says "You must be tired" when I come in and lie back in a chair dead tired."

"Well done! It's bound to improve you. You know what Ruback says. You bring on the experience you need."

"Just because you've cut loose, Sophie!"

"Ah. But think of what I went through first!"

"Yes, but why should I have Philip round my neck now? Is it fair?"

"Oh absolutely! . . . By the way, you didn't mind, did you, about your room? I didn't read a single letter or touch a single book. Just opened a tin of Heinz baked beans—half size."

"I didn't mind. I was flattered, if you want to know. Wish you'd do it again. Isn't it a hole?"

"Marvellous. I loved it. I'm going back to Paris, Guy. My old Languages School is opening a branch there."

"Oh, so we'll see each other. Better not tell Philip. He'll go down another notch if you do. You know he keeps asking me to *explain* things to him. It's all why, why, why? He can't understand what has gone wrong. He says he can't get anything he wants from life. If you ask me, he's going to spend the next five years locked up in a cupboard, trying to sort himself out."

"Please don't tell me about him . . . I really can't bear it, even now. It's so terribly sad. I shall never love anyone else. Do you know what has happened to me, Guy? I no longer want anything from life . . . what I wanted was Philip. And I still want him—as he was in the beginning."

"Stop! It's too intellectual."

His tone was so firm and humorous that I stopped on the spot. All my thoughts floated out of the top of my head. I felt rejuvenated.

"You're better, Guy. You've stopped hissing."

"Oh I only hiss inside now."

We left the road and trod the pure snow on the edge of the Heath. It made a discreet squeak under out feet, like absolutely new cotton-wool wadding being packed into a small space. Everything and every animal on the Heath had been wrapped up and silenced with it. Breath steamed out of us. I said:

"Rudi's taken that operation very well. Like a man."

"Did you think he wouldn't?" asked Guy bitterly.

"That's ungracious of you. He's sixty-eight, Guy … I think you're jealous of him."

"Of *course* I'm jealous of him. You know what the silly old fool has been doing while you've been away? Trying to sack Mrs Wynne. In the end she left him. And after that he had nothing to eat. Literally."

"He could always go to a restaurant or his club."

"Well, when I went to see him he seemed to be living on bread and butter. And then he said he had a boil just under his ear, and pains in his stomach, and he was afraid he was cracking up … And there I was, taking it all in, believing every word. Until he suddenly said he wanted to come to the lectures!"

"Then you saw red!"

"I saw what he was up to. I decided to call his bluff. I said if he really was ill he should call his doctor."

"But he *was* ill …"

Guy pinched his lids together until all I could see was a luminous spasm gliding to and fro inside.

"You can never be sure with Father … even now … I wouldn't swear that appendix was a hundred per cent … it's to punish me for not taking him to the lectures. In any case, I called the doctor … and something very funny happened. You see, Father *had* to come up with some aches and pains, so to begin with he went on about the boil behind his ear."

"I've had boils. They're awful."

"So has the doctor. Because he just pointed at his own ear and said in a cheerful voice: 'Snap!' Then he said—and this is verbatim, it's really beautiful: 'Either they get better, or else they get worse. Or they stay as they are.'!"

"God! Was that National Health?"

"No. Terribly expensive. That makes it all the more beautiful. Well, then he said he'd carry out some tests, and would Father send him a sample? Etc. etc. I think he had an idea it might be diabetes. So what does my father have to do but pee into an old jam-jar that hadn't been properly washed out, and of course the test was positive!"

It was so funny that I had to buffet him on the back to show my appreciation. I said:

"He was determined to get himself into hospital. He really is persevering."

"Well, that's the story of his appendicitis. So does he wonder I don't go and weep all over him! He's as tough as old Nick."

We were going along the path in single file now, exactly as Rudi would have imagined we would go, like Red Indians on the warpath. Guy was in front. It was narrow and the snow was deep-lying on both sides. Walking on an iced cake in the darkness is intoxicating. I felt so fit and uninhibited that when we came under one of the old-fashioned lamps with a snowy canopy on it, I had an overwhelming impulse to make snowballs. I bent down to make one, and Guy saw me just in time, and did the same.

No sooner have you made a snowball than you simply must throw it . . . at a moving target. We began, methodically but gasping with laughter, to pelt one another with snow.

Guy, who was getting the worst of it, slipped, panted and called out:

"Hang on! I'm not Philip, you know." He thought he had found the reason behind my volleys.

"Oh I wouldn't bother to throw them at Philip," I said with the serious knowledgeable disgust of a little girl. I let another one fly off, straight at his head. He ducked (it whizzed into the darkness) and said:

"Well—Sophie, for goodness sake!—who do you think I am?"

Some devil had got into me, and I looked at him fiercely.

"I don't know. Ruback probably."

"What d'you want to throw snowballs at him for?" He was bewildered.

"Because—he's done me so much good, and re-formed me, and I'm grateful—and he's such a great teacher and a good man, that I've simply got to chuck snowballs at him as hard as I can—and serve him *right*!" I paused. "Don't you feel the same, Guy?"

"Well, now you mention it . . ." His flea market coat was white with the gunpowder and debris of my explosions on it.

"You see!"

"But not so hard. *Please*."

"That's the whole point." I ran to some untouched snow. "I've got to throw these snowballs as hard as I can. You see, Guy, I'm not sufficiently developed, thank God, and I'm going to prove it by throwing snowballs."

"Yes, but you're getting vicious." He crouched down.

"Yes I am. I only wish I could put stones in the middle of them."

Smack! One of Guy's hit me on the thigh.

"What a sweet and gentle woman."

"Yes, I'm a dear little thing. Just a womanly woman."

"You certainly are."

"I only wish I'd done this before."

"Well, take that then!"

"Ow! Well, take *that* then!"

"Couldn't you throw them a bit harder? They're only hurting."

"Yes. I can."

Scuffling about on the lamplit path, we used up all our

strength, and only stopped, half-angry, with bits of glittering cold cake stuck to us, when we remembered we would be late for the lecture. *I* was the initiator, and should have been shamefaced. Instead, victorious, stinging all over with blows, I felt I had just broken level with myself. Full of myself, vibrating with myself, I had just regained, with Guy's help, part of the lost territory and pride of a childhood.

⋆ ⋆ ⋆

When I next saw Pussy, it was a week before I left for my new job in Paris. She'd been having rheumatism in her right arm and couldn't afford a physiotherapist to visit her at two guineas an hour so she had to get herself down to the hospital and back. This had tired her very much, and she was behindhand with all her activities.

It was Kate's afternoon off and she let me in herself. Oh how thin she was when she stood up. When I held her for a moment as she kissed me, I felt the bones of her back, (the famous alabaster back) which I had somehow always thought to be the whalebone of her corset.

"Is that you, Pussy?"

"Yes, it's me. I'm getting old. Quickly, in you come. The wind whistles up these stairs, and I've even had to have a heavy curtain put across the door."

We went up to the sitting-room, which was covered with documents. They were on low tables, held down by paperweights. There were two rather shabby wing-chairs in place of the yellow sofa, and the room suddenly seemed much darker than usual. An old-fashioned metal hair-drier was plugged into the wall and had been laid down hugger-mugger on top of the papers. This was part of her domestic life which one did not normally see. It occurred to me that she had begun more and more to live in one room. There was a rug—whose use I could guess from cold days at St Emilion—left tucked into the arm of a chair. Everything had a slight air of decrepitude which I had never noticed before. The gold braid around her cushions, which had always seemed so splendid, was dull and had begun to unravel itself like tufts of hair. It wasn't quite warm enough and I was just going to say so when I sniffed the light taint of burning oil in the air. An oil stove was concealed somewhere, perhaps behind the piano. Melika was economising.

It was like a blow aimed at oneself. I was moved for her and had, for an instant, that smarting pain across the eyes which children feel when they hold back their tears and burn themselves in doing so. Her life had always been so well-cared for and so carefully lived.

I immediately said in an anxious voice:

"You're looking fantastic, as always, Pussy."

One glance in return from those famous eyes, so sweet, much too wise, stopped my blundering nonsense.

"Thank you," she said courteously. No contented growl.

"Shall I bring the hot water in?" I asked.

"No. Certainly not. It won't take me a moment."

I'd made a second mistake. I was trying to help her; a thing I had never done in my life before. She responded as Rudi had done when I once helped him on with his coat. "I'm not an old man yet, you know," he said quickly.

When she returned with the water, her movements were lighter and faster. This made me still more uneasy. And I knew that I must throw myself down in the best chair and be as young and selfish as I had always been. It was the only way in which I could reassure her that during the winter which was now over she had not suddenly grown old.

Tea had been laid out with the same care as before; fresh lace tray-cloth, polished silver, and little cakes with silver balls on them. Ah, so things were all right after all. It was just that I had been travelling and had an altered perspective.

I sat with a gawkishness I knew was elegant, and let her re-live through my limbs certain attitudes she could not now take up herself. Even so, I couldn't help looking around me, again and again, asking myself whether this room was in fact the great stronghold to which all my thoughts had returned in times of anxiety? Yes, this was the place where they came for strength and advice. Somewhere between the piano and the cakes was the spot where, in the past, the magic had been absolutely reliable. Strong enough to take me to Brighton, and then to Normandy, and through the streets of Paris, and home once more, with a feeling that I had something solid inside me again and could go forward.

We gossiped.

"Pussy, what's all this about Rudi's appendix? Was it necessary?"

"Of course it was. Absolutely essential. Who on earth told you that it wasn't?"

"Well ... Guy thinks it's just another way of getting at him. It's one of Rudi's 'tricks' to get his own way."

"We all know *that*. Rudi has to have what he wants. He lives in the present, thank God. What a gift! And he was born with it!"

"He's rather jealous of you at the moment."

"Rudi is?"

I had struck gold; she looked really pleased; the sweet hot tea was melting us.

"He says you're as thick as thieves with Mr Ruback."

"Because he came to tea *once*! Really! So he's jealous. Well, well. I'm very glad to hear it. Once I had vetted Mr Ruback I, for one, was perfectly happy. Let me tell you that he is a man in a million; just like Ziz. His range and his interpretation are—out of this world."

She began to hold forth about Mr Ruback, and I listened amazed, as though I had never met him and had never been to his lectures. An entirely new, rather Russian figure emerged ... crossing the steppes in a cloak and top boots, with a sunrise behind him ...

As she spoke out warmly, the room began to put itself together in the old way. It grew lighter and larger. The Yorkshire terrier woke up and took part. I saw that the design on the plates in green and gold had something unique to it that I remembered I had very much liked. She was just about to set the final seal of her approval on Mr Ruback, and had lifted up her head and cleared her throat to do so, when I realised with a start that one essential ingredient was missing to this great symphony of moral inspiration ... the brooch with the slab of green marble in it.

"Pussy! Your brooch—do put it on!" I called out suddenly.

She put her hand to the empty spot and blushed.

"My brooch? I ... sold it. It never really suited me. Much too heavy. When your neck gets older you want something lightweight there."

"Oh Pussy. What a loss."

"Not at all. I happened to want fifty pounds. I don't believe in hoarding things up. I'd much rather take a holiday. And everything's going up. It's different for people who are earning an income, like you, Sophie."

"Oh Pussy."

"Don't be sentimental."

"I can't help it."

"Stop it at once. It's revolting."

"Why do you always make me cry?" But I knew the reason.

It was because she loved me; I could feel it physically. And there's nothing that so quickly undermines you.

"You're making yourself cry. You know you always use me as your psychoanalyst. That reminds me! You came into some money, I hear? Tell me about it."

"Oh—it keeps shrinking. Death duties have to be paid. And then, if I invest it, it turns out I'll get hardly anything at all."

"That's typical! You'd be much better off with a brooch or two. They don't shrink. And they're there when you want them. Now ... let's see. What time is it? *Nearly* six. You know what I think we both deserve? Just a splash of vodka. You can get it out of the corner cupboard for me ... And don't you dare to say 'Oh Pussy' like that to me again, and make big eyes at me. Just when you're about to start a new life."